About the Author

Elizabeth Kelly is a historical fiction author best known for The Tudors Series. She is a former teacher with a degree in Ancient History and Archaeology and is fascinated by historical research. She enjoys travelling to see places of historical interest including the Pyramids, the Great Wall of China and the medieval abbeys of England. She was inspired to start writing historical fiction after taking several online courses in creative writing during the lockdown. She is a highly imaginative writer who loves to create an escape into the alternative reality of creative fiction. She lives in Yorkshire.

<u>The Tudors Series</u>

(1) The Tudor Maid (the story of the seamstress Margery Hallows).
(2) The Tudor Lady in Waiting (the story of Lady Margaret de la Roche).
(3) The Tudor Fool: My Life with Henry VIII (the story of Will Somers).
(4) The Dark Lady: The Rise and Fall of Queen Anne Boleyn.
(5) The Shadow of the Tower (the story of Lady Margaret Pole).

This book is dedicated to my family.

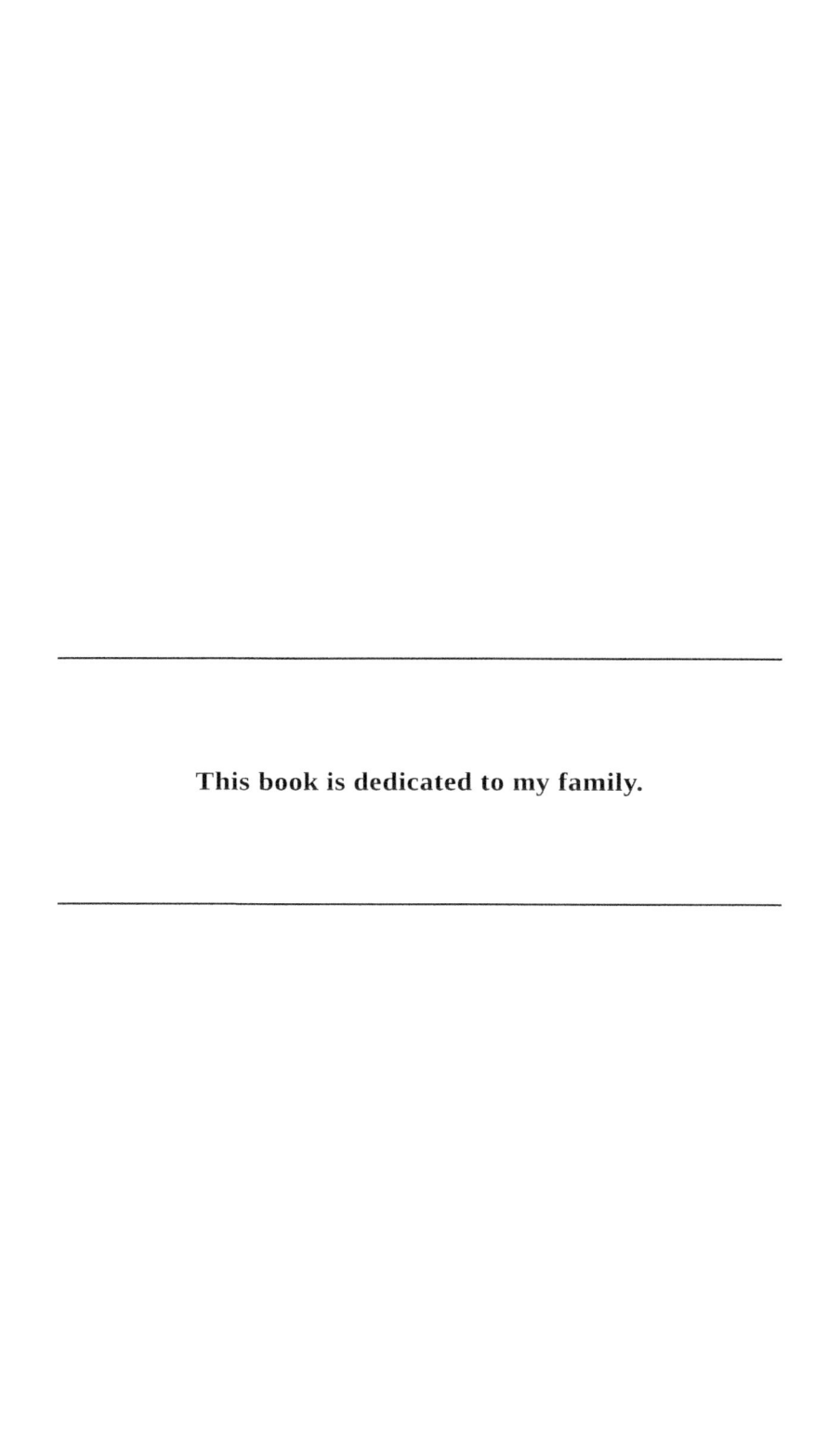

THE QUEEN'S VAGABOND

AUTHOR: ELIZABETH KELLY

ILLUSTRATOR: JULIA BAI

Copyright©2024 by Elizabeth Kelly

Illustrator: Julia Bai

All rights reserved. No part of this publication may be reproduced, distributed or transmitted in any form or by any means, including photocopying, recording, or other electronic or mechanical methods, without the prior written permission of the publisher, except in the case of brief quotations embodied in critical reviews and certain other noncommercial uses permitted by copyright law.

List of Historical Characters

The Family of Nathan Field
The Family of Nathan Field
Nathan Field, former scholar at St Paul's Grammar School (1587-1620)
Reverend John Field, his father
Mistress Joan Field, his mother
Reverend Theophilus Field, Bishop of Llandaff, his brother
Nathaniel Field, his brother
Richard Mulcaster, headmaster of St Paul's Grammar School

The Masters of the Children of the Queen's Revels
Master Nathaniel Giles
Master Henry Evans
Master Thomas Kendall
Master Robert Keysar

The Players of the Children of the Queen's Revels
Jack Underwood
William Ostler
Saloman Pavy, former apprentice to the choirmaster at St Paul's Chapel.
Philip Pykman, former apprentice to Richard Chambers.
Thomas Grimes, former apprentice to Richard Chambers.
Alvery Trussell, former apprentice to Thomas Giles.
Abell Cooke, apprentice.
James Bristowe
Thomas Morton
Robert Baxter.

Playwrights

Christopher Marlowe

William Shakespeare

Mistress Anne Hathaway, his wife

Ben Jonson

Samuel Daniel

Francis Beaumont

John Fletcher

Philip Massinger

Actors and Managers

Edward Alleyn

Richard Burbage

Philip Henslowe

John Heminges

The Royal Court

Queen Elizabeth I (1533 -1603)

King James I (1603-1625)

Queen Anna of Denmark (1603-1619)

Lord Salisbury, Robert Cecil, the Lord Treasurer (1563-1612)

Lord Essex, Robert Devereux

Sir Gelly Merrick

Sir Walter Raleigh

Wat Raleigh, his son

Lord Somerset, Robert Carr, the king's favourite

The duke of Buckingham, George Villiers, the king's favourite

Lord Argyll, Archibald Campbell (the seventh earl)

Lady Anne Argyll, his wife

Sir Edmund Tilney, Master of the Revels 1579-1610

Sir George Buck, Master of the Revels 1610-1622

Lord Hunsdon, Henry Carey, patron of the Lord Chamberlain's Men, Lord Chamberlain 1585-1596

Lord Cobham, William Brooke, Lord Chamberlain 1596-1597

Lord Hunsdon, George Carey, Lord Chamberlain 1597- 1603

Lord Thomas Howard, earl of Suffolk, Lord Chamberlain 1603-1614

Lord Somerset, Robert Carr, Lord Chamberlain 1614-1615

Lord Pembroke, William Herbert, Lord Chamberlain 1615-1625

Historical Notes on the Text

(1) The popularity of stage plays led to the building of the Rose, Swan and Globe Theatres in London between 1587 and 1598. They were built in Southwark outside the boundaries of the city.

(2) A body of legislation was issued to control the acting profession: A proclamation of 1559 forbade plays to discuss any matters of religion or government; The Vagabonds Act of 1572 ordered that any unlicensed vagabonds were to be whipped and burned through the ear; In 1574, the Mayor of London prohibited the performance of plays within the city limits; The Blasphemy Act of 1606 imposed a ban upon swearing on the stage or taking the Lord's name in vain; In 1642 the theatres were closed for eighteen years for promoting "*lascivious mirth and levity.*"

(3) In December 1601 Henry Clifton, a gentleman from Norfolk put forward a Bill of Complaint against "Giles, Evans, Robinson and others." He accused them of abducting his son Thomas Clifton on his way to Christ Church grammar school on 13th December 1600. Henry Clifton stated that seven other boys were also "unjustly taken" around the same time. Their names were: John Chappell, John Motteram and Nathan Field, who were grammar school boys; Alvery Trussell, an apprentice to Thomas Gyles; Philip Pykman and Thomas Grymes, apprentices to Richard and George Chambers; and Saloman Pavey, apprentice to Edward Pearce the choirmaster at St. Pauls. Consequently, Henry Evans was censured for "*taking up of gentlemen's children against their wills and to employ them for players.*"

(4) Alice Cooke apprenticed her son Abell to Thomas Kendall for

three years in November 1606. However, Abell left the company in May 1607.

(5) Philip Henslowe bought a boy named James Bristowe to act as a player in his company in 1597. He paid £8 for him.

(6) Nicholas Odell wrote the comic English play *"Ralph Roister Doister"* based upon the Roman plays of Plautus and Terence.

(7) Ben Jonson owed the staging his play *"Every Man in His Humour"* to the intervention of William Shakespeare. It was performed at the Globe theatre by the Lord Chamberlain's Men in 1598:

"His Acquaintance with Ben Jonson began with a remarkable piece of Humanity and good Nature; Mr. Jonson, who was at that Time altogether unknown to the World, had offer'd one of his Plays to the Players, in order to have it Acted; and the Persons into whose Hands it was put, after having turn'd it carelessly and superciliously over, were just upon returning it to him with an ill-natur'd Answer, that it would be of no service to their Company, when Shakespeare luckily cast his Eye upon it, and found something so well in it as to engage him first to read it through, and afterwards to recommend Mr. Jonson and his Writings to the Publick. After this they were profess'd Friends" (Nicholas Rowe, Some Account of the Life of Mr. William Shakespeare, 1709).

(8) The performance of *"Richard II"* with its controversial abdication scene took place at the Globe theatre on 7th February 1601 on the eve of the Essex rebellion. Queen Elizabeth had the play performed before her at court. But no action was taken against the players of the Lord Chamberlain's Men or its author William Shakespeare.

(9)   The earl of Southampton joined the rebellion which was led by the earl of Essex in 1601. He was imprisoned in the Tower of London. But he had the company of his pet cat Trixie. *"After he had been confined there a small time, he was surprised by a visit from his favourite cat, which had found its way to the Tower; and, as tradition says, reached its master by descending the chimney of his apartment"* (Thomas Pennant, Some Account of London, 1793).

(10)   In 1602 the duke of Stettin-Pomerania attended a performance at Blackfriars theatre: *"For a whole hour preceding the play one listens to a delightful musical entertainment on organs, lutes, pandorins, mandolins, violins and flutes, as on the present occasion, indeed, when a boy cum voce tremulo sang so charmingly to the accompaniment of a bass-viol that unless possibly the nuns at Milan may have excelled him, we had not heard his equal on our journey"* (The diary of Philip Julius, duke of Stettin-Pomerania, as kept during his visit to London in 1602 by his tutor and secretary, Frederic Gerschow).

(11)   Ben Jonson told William Drummond in 1619 that *"Nid Field was his Schollar and he had read to him the Satyres of Horace and some Epigrames of Martiall"* (Informations to William Drummond of Hawthornden, 1711).

(12)   In August 1605 Ben Jonson and George Chapman were imprisoned for offending King James I: *"He was delated by Sr James Murray to the King for writting something against the Scots jn a play Eastward hoe and voluntarily imprissonned himself with Chapman and Marston, who had written it amongst him. The report was that they should then had their ears cutt and noses. After their delivery he banqueted all his friends"* (Informations to William Drummond of Hawthornden, 1711).

(13) The writer John Aubrey recorded that the playwrights Francis Beaumont and John Fletcher *"lived on the bankside, not far from the playhouse, both bachelors who lay together; had one wench in the house between them, which they did so admire; and had the same clothes and cloak between them"* (John Aubrey, Brief Lives, 1669-1696).

(14) The writer Thomas Fuller wrote that John Fletcher was accused of treason after he was overheard discussing a play: *"Meeting once in a tavern, to contrive the rough draft of a tragedy (The Maid's Tragedy by Beaumont and Fletcher) Fletcher undertook the kill the king; whose words being overheard by a listener… he was accused of high treason"* (Thomas Fuller, The History of the Worthies of England, 1662).

(15) In 1616 Princess Pocahontas and her husband John Rolfe travelled from Virginia to London and attended a masque at Whitehall Palace.

(16) In 1616 Jonson was appointed as the first poet laureate in England with a royal pension of £100 a year.

(17) A week before Shakespeare's death in April 1616, Ben Jonson and Michael Drayton went to visit him in Stratford: *"Shakespeare, Drayton, and Ben Jonson had a merry meeting and, it seems, drank too hard, for Shakespeare died of a fever there contracted."* (The diary entry of John Ward, the vicar of Stratford written in 1662).

(18) On 29th June 1613 the Globe Theatre burned down during a performance of *"All Is True"* by William Shakespeare: *"All is True, representing some principal pieces of the reign of Henry VIII, which set forth with many extraordinary circumstances of*

pomp and majesty even to the matting of the stage; the knights of the order with their Georges and Garter, the guards with their embroidered coats, and the like; sufficient in truth within awhile to make greatness very familiar, if not ridiculous. Now King Henry making a masque at the Cardinal Wolsey's house, and certain cannons being shot off at his entry, some of the paper or other stuff, wherewith one of them was stopped, did light on the thatch, where, being thought at first but idle smoak, and their eyes more attentive to the show, it kindled inwardly, and ran round like a train, consuming within less than an hour the whole house to the very ground. This was the fatal period of that virtuous fabrick, wherein yet nothing did perish but wood and straw, and a few forsaken cloaks; only one man had his breeches set on fire, that would perhaps have broyled him, if he had not, by the benefit of a provident wit, put it out with a bottle of ale" (Letter of Sir Henry Watton, 1613).

(19) William Trumbull, Ambassador to Holland, reported that *"the earl of Argyll has paid for the nursing of a child, which the world sayes is the daughter to my lady and Nathan Field, the player"* (Letter of William Trumbull to Lord Hay, 1619).

(20) There were numerous outbreaks of plague in sixteenth and seventeenth century London. They culminated in the Great Plague of 1665-1666 which killed 100, 000 people.

Contents

Chapter 1: The Scholar (1600) 9

Chapter 2: Life at the Blackfriars Theatre 29

Chapter 3: The Court of the Faerie Queene 41

Chapter 4: The Boy Actor 57

Chapter 5: The Accession of King James I (1603) 73

Chapter 6: The Jacobean Court 87

Chapter 7: The Dangers of Satire 103

Chapter 8: Interlude in a Prison 111

Chapter 9: The Gunpowder Plot (5th November 1505) 121

Chapter 10: The Playwright 133

Chapter 11: The Lady Elizabeth's Men 151

Chapter 12: The King's Men 169

Chapter 13: The Toast of London 187

Chapter 14: The Star-Crossed Lovers 199

Chapter 15: Fallen from Heaven 215

Epilogue 223

Book Group Discussion Guide 225

Select Bibliography 227

CHAPTER 1

The Scholar
(1600)

"Taking up gentlemen's children against their wills and employing them as players"

(The Court of the Star Chamber, 1602).

"The stage doth stain pure gentle blood."

(John Davies of Hereford, Microcosmos, 1603).

My name is Nathan Field, the famous actor and playwright. I was thought to be an unlucky child by my family, for I was born after the death of my father. But for my part, I regarded myself as being fortunate. It is certain that my life would otherwise never have taken the path that it did. For my father, John Field, was a famous Puritan preacher. After his funeral, my mother was left a widow with seven children to support. Out of consideration for my father's virtues and my mother's necessity, I was offered a place at St Paul's Grammar School in London. It was only half a mile from where we lived on Grub Street near Moorgate. I was eligible for a free place since I was a bright boy without a father to support him. My older brother Theophilus had taught me how to read and write in English and Latin. My mother hoped that I would follow in his footsteps and gain a place to study at Oxford University. He intended to follow a career in the church like our father. I was one of the best pupils in the school, despite my youth. I had a clear voice for reciting my lessons and a retentive memory.

The headmaster, Master Richard Mulcaster, had an excellent reputation as a scholar. He taught Greek, Latin, oratory and rhetoric. He also believed in the value of plays for teaching moral values and building confidence in his pupils. Accordingly, he wrote a comic play called *"Ralph Roister-Doister"* about the misadventures of a foolish, swaggering boy. He cast me as the lead player and spent many hours coaching me in the role, The performance was a great success and I felt elated by my triumph. After the performance, he introduced me to his guest. Master Henry Evans had a pleasant countenance and a charming smile. He wore a splendid doublet and hose of russet velvet in which he cut an impressive figure. I made my bow as Master Mulcaster had taught me. He nodded approvingly.

"Very creditable, Nathan," he remarked. "Do you like performing in plays?"

"Yes Sir, very much," I replied enthusiastically. I hoped that my headmaster would choose me to star in his next play. He turned to Master Mulcaster who was watching him closely.

"He is everything that you said he was," he said eagerly. "He has real potential and I'm very interested."

Master Mulcaster smiled broadly. I had never seen him look so contented. "Then we must discuss the matter further," he replied. "Very well, Nathan, you may go home now."

I rushed home to tell my mother all about my triumph. But she was not as impressed as I had expected her to be.

"I don't know what your father would have said, Nat," she said disapprovingly. "You know he was a preacher and he thought that plays were immoral."

"But my headmaster wrote it," I protested. "And it is a very moral story in which the virtuous are rewarded and the wicked are punished."

"Well, if it is part of your education then I cannot object to it," she conceded. "I only hope that nothing bad will come of it."

"Of course it won't, Mother," I assured her impatiently. I was disappointed that she thought so little of my achievement. If only she had witnessed the admiration of my headmaster and his guest, I was certain that she would have been more impressed.

However, her prophecy was fulfilled only too soon. The following week as I was making my way to school, two burly men stepped into my path. It was November and the mornings were as dark as night-time. Their faces were obscured by shadows and their bulky figures blocked the road ahead. Fear surged through my veins and I quickly looked about me. But there was nowhere for me to take refuge.

"Is your name Nathan?" one of them demanded. He brandished a lantern in my face and it cast an eerie light upon the cobblestones.

My heart raced. "Who are you?" I stammered; my voice barely audible.

"He's the one for certain," the other man declared. "He matches the description perfectly. Come with us, boy."

He grabbed me by the arms and lifted me up. I kicked and shouted, but my protests were futile. The streets were deserted at that hour. There was no-one around to see or hear me. I was wrapped in a rough cloak and carried away through the streets of London like a sack of cabbages. My abductor ran through the streets gripping me tightly around the waist. I tried to kick him and he slapped my legs hard. My cries were muffled by the thick fabric around my face. I wondered where he was taking me and what would become of me. Perhaps I would be bundled on board a ship and taken on a voyage to a distant land. Would anyone every know what had become of me?

Finally, we arrived at the Blackfriars theatre. Master Henry Evans awaited us, a man full of authority and deceit. He examined me, assessing my worth.

"Yes, he is the one," he told the men and handed one of them a purse. He stuffed it into his sleeve with a smirk and they vanished into the darkness. The door behind me slammed shut and I heard the latch fall into place. There was no way out.

"I haven't done anything!" I protested, my voice echoing around the entrance chamber. My heart was hammering in my chest. I wondered what was going to happen next.

Master Evans raised his hand, silencing me. "No accusations, boy," he said. "You have been chosen for a great honour. The Children of the Chapel Royal await you!"

"I can't be an actor," I objected. "My family will never allow it." I had no desire to leave my grammar school. I wanted to complete my education. Scholars were highly respected, but everyone looked down on players. They were despised as beggars and vagabonds.

"Your family will have no choice in the matter," he said firmly. "I have the right to impress anyone into our ranks."

"And if I refuse?" I challenged.

His eyes bore into mine. "Displease me, and you'll learn the consequences. I am your new master now."

"Who said so?" I demanded.

I manage a company of boy actors," he explained. "You are now a member of my company and must follow my orders. This is my theatre and you will perform here once a week when you have been trained. You will be living here and everything will be provided for you." And so, my fate was sealed and I was swept into the world of the theatre. I was too bewildered to make any further complaint.

"Come with me," ordered Master Evans. He took me into the theatre which had a stage at one end, two galleries on each side and rows of benches which filled the hall. It was illuminated by two great chandeliers which hung from the ceiling. I had never been inside a playhouse before and I stared in wonder at the sight. An older boy was directing a rehearsal of twenty other boys on the stage. They varied in age from twelve to sixteen and they were all dressed in scarlet livery. Their eyes fastened upon me at once.

I heard an excited whisper. "He's the new one!"

"I trust the rehearsals are progressing well, Thomas?" enquired Master Evans genially.

"Yes, Master Evans," he replied.

"Excellent!" he said. "I trust the company are ready to astound me with their prowess. You may take Nathan up the dormitory. He has just joined our company!"

"Welcome to Blackfriars, Nathan," said Thomas. "The dormitory is up the stairs. Follow me." At the top of the staircase was a large room lined with pallets. A set of livery was lying neatly folded on the pallet nearest to the door. I realised that my arrival here today had been a carefully arranged plan.

"That's for you," said Thomas. "Put it on." I reluctantly took off my scholar's uniform and dressed myself in the heavy woollen livery. The scarlet colour made me into highly conspicuous figure.

"You'll have to take care not to spoil it or you'll be sure to hear about it from Master Evans," he remarked. "We have to look neat and clean at all times. Master Evans is not a bad sort. But he only cares about one thing." *Making a profit*, I thought.

Thomas placed the cap on my head and adjusted it. "Now you are one of us. Remember, there is no use running away. You would be recognised at once and brought back. And then the masters would punish you." I bit my lip. It seemed that there was no recourse for me.

"You were a grammar school boy, weren't you?" he said.

"St Paul's school," I replied proudly.

He nodded his head. "Yes, the masters prefer choristers and scholars. They learn to perform more quickly. But they cannot take too many or complaints will arise." I thought back to Master Evans' visit to St Pauls. He must have made an agreement about me with Master Mulcaster. My heart burned within me. I had admired my headmaster. But he had sold me as if I was a valuable dog that he had trained.

"What about my mother?" I protested. "She will wonder where I am."

"Master Evans will write her a letter," he informed me. "He will tell her that you have been selected to join the Children of the Chapel Royal and that he is now your master. Your uniform will be sent back to her along with the rest of your things. Unless you have something that you wish to keep?"

"My books," I said instantly. In my satchel I had my copies of William Lyly's *Latin Grammar*, Plutarch's *"Lives of the Noble Greeks and Romans"* and Ovid's *"Metamorphoses."* They were the most valuable things I owned.

"Put them under your pillow," he said. "There isn't any space in here for chests."

A chorus of *re, mi, fa, sol, la* floated up the stairs. Thomas cocked his head to the side to listen. "Ah, now they are getting into tune for the musical interlude!" he remarked. "The playgoers enjoy the novelty of children who can sing, play and dance so these are included in all the performances. Master Giles teaches us how to sing songs and airs," he explained. "He is the master of the choristers of the Chapel Royal. He instructs us how to sing in chorus and perform solos, duets and quartets in parts. I hope for your sake that you have a passable voice."

I said nothing. At school I had learned the liberal arts of Latin grammar, arithmetic, logic, rhetoric and oratory. But not singing.

"Master Rosseter teaches music and dancing," he continued. "He is one of the queen's own lute-players. And we are taught how to perform by Master Evans. We have rehearsals every morning and lessons in the afternoon. On Saturdays we will give public performances as soon as Master Evans thinks we are ready."

He noticed my downcast expression. "In the evenings we may play cards in the dining room or read in the dormitory as long as we have learned our parts for the next day. It is a busy life. And it will be even busier for you."

"Why is that?" I enquired.

"You are the newest member of the company," he explained. "So, you will be responsible for taking care of the dormitory. The pallets have to be changed every morning. And once a week, you will have to sweep up the reeds and scrub the floor with soap and water. Then you put fresh reeds down."

I scowled for I had never done such tasks before. "That's women's work!" I objected.

"No women are allowed to come in here," he replied. "We are a boys' company. But I wouldn't fret over it. Master Evans will be recruiting another boy soon and he will take over the duties. I'll take you down to the hall now and you can watch the rest of the rehearsals."

I spent the rest of the morning observing Master Evans direct the company in "*Ralph Roister-Doister*." It had evidently caught his fancy. At least this was familiar to me. When the rehearsal ended, we went upstairs to the dining room.

"You sit at the end of the bench, Nathan," said Thomas.

"Such a pretty boy!" said Robert sarcastically. "He's sure to play the female roles!" The boy actors played the male and female parts on the stage. Respectable women did not even speak in public, let alone act on the stage.

I shared a trencher with a young boy named Alvery. He was delighted by my arrival. It meant he could relinquish his duties in the dormitory. "It makes you late for breakfast," he warned me. "Sometimes you miss it altogether!"

"Hush!" said Thomas. "We will say Grace." The boys bowed their heads. Then the two oldest boys, Thomas and Robert, took charge of serving the food. Master Evans often delegated his duties to them if he was called away or busy in the office. They taught new boys the basics of reading, declaiming, music and dancing. Thomas was a good teacher, but Robert had no patience. However, he was very adept at the card, dice and chess games we played in the evenings. Our food was bread, cheese and pottage, but it was not as good as my mother made it. Nor was it as plentiful for our masters did not allow us to have second helpings. On Fridays and Saturdays, we ate fish and on Sundays we had salt beef. Our drink was small beer, but it was often sour. The older boys muttered that Master Kenyon got it cheap from the local taverns instead of buying it freshly brewed.

A short time later a bell rang noisily. "We have to go down to the schoolroom now, Nathan," said Thomas. "It is time for the music lesson. Come with me."

Master Rosseter was a scholarly man who wore the same scarlet livery as the company. It signified that he was one of the queen's servants. Thomas introduced me.

"Here is our new player, Master Rosseter."

"Indeed," he replied. "Can you read music and play an instrument?"

"No, Master Rosseter," I admitted.

"Very well," he sighed with irritation. "Thomas, fetch a recorder and teach him the notes and the fingering."

A great deal of time was spent in practising music. The boys started on the recorder and then progressed onto the lute, the mandolin, the violin and the flute. Some of them had even mastered the bass-viola, cello and cornet. Soon a great cacophony erupted as the boys began to play on their instruments. Master Thomas took me away to a quiet corner of the hall. I spent the following hour practising finger exercises. Then the company assembled in the hall for a lesson in dancing.

"Saloman, strike up the lute for the galliard," Master Rosseter ordered. "We will take partners to practice our steps." At once the boys moved into pairs.

"Make your courtesies," he cried. "And now begin!" I was partnered by a boy of similar height. I did my best to keep in step with him, but it was a clumsy attempt. He scowled at me.

Master Rosseter shook his head. "Thomas and Robert, come forward and demonstrate," he said impatiently. "The rest of you watch their steps carefully. See how they move with grace like courtiers!"

Saloman struck up again. He was a most accomplished lute-player for such a young boy. He was a former member of the choir of the Chapel Royal and the best singer and musician in the company. He told us that the lives of the choristers were even more restricted and onerous. They were obliged to attend services in the chapel every morning and evening. They had constant rehearsals in singing and music in order to learn new anthems and motets. And they were expected to master both the lute and the organ.

"It is far easier to be an apprentice than a chorister," he sighed. "At least they can rest in the evenings. Often the court composers would bring their compositions to Master Giles at the last minute. Then we would have to practice a new piece of music late into the night in order to sing it perfectly the following morning. To make matters worse, the Master of the Revels demanded our services in performing in the court masques. Christmas and Easter were the worst times of all. We had to sing the choral services in the chapel during the day and then entertain the court at night. We barely had any time to eat or sleep."

"What is a masque?" I asked him.

"It is a new form of entertainment," he replied. "It combines dancing, music, drama, scenery and costumes into one overall theme. But it is so costly that only the queen or her wealthiest nobles can afford to commission them. So, they are normally only performed at the court."

The following morning, I joined the rest of the company for the morning rehearsal. Master Evans was continuing to work on speeches and scenes from "*Ralph Roister-Doister.*" Today he was keen to show me off to Master Giles.

"Nathan, you may demonstrate your comic talents to the company," he declared. "Come out to the front."

Reluctantly I stood up and came forward. The other boys looked surprised that such attention was being paid to a new boy. Master Giles looked equally forbidding. But Master Evans' face was wreathed in smiles. "In this play the trickster Matthew Merrygreek urges Ralph to try to win the hand of Dame Custance," he said. "He persuades him to send her a letter written by a scrivener. But when Ralph's suit is rejected, he vows to take his revenge on him! Nathan, kindly declaim your speech about a thousand wives from Act Three, Scene Four."

I had performed it quite recently, so the text was still fresh in my memory. I took a deep breath and spoke with all the vigour I could muster:

"Yes, for although he had as many lives,
As a thousande widowes, and a thousande wives,
As a thousande lions, and a thousand rattes,
A thousande wolves, and a thousande cattes,
A thousande bulles, and a thousande calves,
And a thousande legions divided in halves,

He shall never scape death on my swordes point,
Though I shoulde be torne therefore joint by joint."

Master Evans beamed. "Yes, Master Mulcaster taught you well, Nathan!" he observed. "But we shall teach you even better. Here at Blackfriars, you shall achieve your full potential for the stage! As all of you will do! Now, Robert that is your cue to present your speech as Merrygreeke."

Robert shot me a black look. It was plain that he did not intend to be upstaged by a mere newcomer. He made his reply promptly and I could see that he was a confident performer:

"Nay, if ye will kill him, I will not fetch him,
I will not in so muche extremity sette him,
He may yet amende sir, and be an honest man,
Therefore, pardon him good soule, as muche as ye can."

"Excellent, boys!" he declared. Now we need Dame Custance so that we can take the scene from the beginning. Jack, step forward and join the others."

In this manner, Master Evans built the speeches into scenes and the scenes into acts. His enthusiasm was contagious and he encouraged us to find the humour in the scenes. "Playgoers come to the theatre to be entertained!" he reminded us. "They don't wish to see long faces on the stage. Now remember, what should you do if you happen to forget your line?

"Improvise another that will make sense in the dialogue," replied Robert promptly.

Master Giles snorted. "Master Evans, you are teaching these boys bad habits. They must learn to speak their lines just as the playwright wrote them!"

"Quite so, Master Giles," Master Evans agreed. "It is only a remedy for dire extremities and no excuse for laziness."

We continued rehearsing the play for the rest of that week and into the following week. Master Evans and Master Giles were both present to supervise our efforts. I noticed that the former apprentice boys had the most difficulty in mastering their speeches. They were barely literate and so they struggled to read their parts and declaim them. They had been selected for their good looks rather than their skills. Suddenly, our practice was interrupted by a loud commotion at the door. I heard shouts and wondered what was happening. But Master Evan's face brightened with expectation. Two men entered the hall holding a boy about the same age as myself. He was dressed in a school uniform, but he was not a scholar of St Paul's. Instead, he wore the badge of Christ Church grammar school. I recognised the men as the same ones who had taken me. Clearly, they had seized another boy on his way to school in the same way.

Master Evans smiled broadly when he saw him. "Thomas, welcome to the Blackfriars theatre. This is your new home. You have been recommended to me as a suitable talent for the stage. My name is Master Evans and I am the manager of the company."

Thomas looked no more pleased at this news than I had been. "My father doesn't want me to be an actor," he protested. "He wants me to go to university and study the law!"

"It makes no difference what he wants. I am your master now," said Master Evans dismissively. "Robert, take our new player to the dormitory."

Thomas gave up his protests and followed Robert up the stairs. My mind was in a whirl. So, Master Morton had been right. The masters were taking more boys to add to the company. I felt sorry for Thomas, but I was pleased for myself. Now he would have to scrub the floor of the dormitory every week!

However, the abduction of Thomas had a sequel. When he failed to come home after school, his father went looking for him. Before nightfall he had traced him to Blackfriars. He seething with rage by the time he arrived at the theatre. He hammered on the door demanding to be let in. Master Evans' men opened the door and he pushed them aside.

"Where is my son?" he shouted. "Hand him over at once, you rogue! How dare you lay hands on a gentleman's son!"

Master Evans frowned. He wasn't used to being challenged in his own domain. "Take care how you address me, my good man," he retorted. "I hold a licence from the queen to recruit suitable boys for my company. I have the right to take as many boys as I please."

Master Clifton spluttered with indignation. "Thomas is no pauper to be snatched from the streets. He is my only son and heir and he is not for the stage. I have better plans for him than to spend his life as a common player. It would dishonour my family name. The Cliftons are Norfolk gentlefolk and he shall follow a respectable profession."

Master Evans folded his arms. "I shall not give him up for all your protestations. But you will live to be thankful to me. Your son has a great opportunity as one of the Children of the Chapel Royal. My actors receive an excellent training. Thomas will have a splendid future on the stage. Many fathers would be glad to see their sons so well established in life."

Master Clifton's face turned puce. "My son has been unjustly taken. And he shall not be basely used for your corrupt gain. He is no suitable apprentice for you. He is a scholar, not a chorister. He has no skill in singing nor in sight-reading. I have friends who will not stand by and see me wronged in such a manner. Hand him over at once or it will be the worse for you!"

"Friend, I will show you exactly what I can do," he replied blandly. "Come here, Thomas." The boy stepped forward gladly, thinking his deliverance was sure. Master Evans handed him a parchment and he looked at it in dismay.

"You will take this part and spend the next hour learning it perfectly. If you do not, then you will be whipped for disobedience. Do you understand me sirrah?"

The boy nodded miserably. "Then away with you to the dormitory at once," he ordered. "You are one of my apprentices and I have no intention of relinquishing you." Thomas gave his father a despairing look. Then he dropped his head and slowly walked away.

His father clenched his fists. "By the rood, you have not heard the last of this matter. I will have my boy again in spite of what you say. And if you lay a hand on him, I shall see you in the pillory!"

Master Evans gave a cold smile. "So, you say, Master Clifton, but this is my theatre and your son is now my apprentice. He will follow my orders or suffer the consequences. You can complain to whomever you want, but it won't matter a jot. I have taken Thomas legally and my authority comes from the queen. I am merely carrying out my duty to the crown."

"Duty?" he snapped. "You talk to me of duty? You are no more than a villain to abduct honest men's children in this way. You will be sorry for it, I promise you. You shall hear from my friends and it will not be to your liking!" He walked out and slammed the door.

Master Evans snorted. "Empty words. He will soon find out that he has no recourse against me." He was confident that Master Clifton would soon give up his demands. But that was not the end of the matter. A fortnight later a messenger arrived bearing a letter addressed to Master Evans. When he broke the seal, he stiffened with alarm. He hurried across the chamber and brandished the missive in the face of Master Giles.

"That varlet Clifton has made good on his threat," he burst out, his voice trembling. "He does have powerful friends. This is a bill of complaint signed by Sir John Fortescue, the Chancellor of the Exchequer. What shall we do?"

Master Giles snatched the document from his grasp. He quickly scanned the lines and I watched as his brow furrowed. "Hold your nerve, man," he advised in a gruff voice. "Let him go to court for his son. We hold a license from the queen herself!"

But the doughty Master Clifton succeeded in his suit. Master Evans was censured for taking gentlemen's children and using them as players. He was dismissed from his post as manager. I wondered if my own liberation was imminent. Would I, too, be released? But it was only the fortunate Thomas Clifton who regained his freedom. My own family weighed heavily on my mind. Surely, they would not want me to join a company of players. I longed for Theophilus to come and reclaim me and put me back in school. But he was away in Cambridge. *Would my mother come and demand my return?* I imagined her face, etched with anxiety and concern. But the days lengthened into weeks and nobody intervened on my behalf. My hope gradually faded into disappointment. *Resign yourself*, I whispered to my trembling heart. Master Giles, resilient as an ancient oak, retained his position. The Children of the Chapel continued to tread the boards. But no more boys were impressed into service. Instead, they were apprenticed as in any other trade.

Master Kendall replaced Master Evans as the manager of the company. He was a haberdasher who supplied the company with their costumes. At first, I was pleased that Master Evans had got his just deserts, for he was clearly a rogue. But I did not rejoice for long. Master Kendall was as tall and thin as a poker. He wore a black cloak which reached down to his feet. He was a stern man who was entirely lacking in humour. I could not imagine a greater contrast to the ebullient and colourful Master Evans. The masters were greatly discomfited by the departure of Thomas Clifton. I overheard them muttering together: "But none of the other boys are leaving. They don't have any Privy Councillors up their sleeves!" However, they soon had a further setback when James Cutler's voice suddenly went off. He was now entirely unfit for the stage. So, he was issued with a new suit and released from the company.

"The company is badly understrength, Master Giles," complained Master Kendall. "It is imperative that we recruit another boy. I shall make some enquires."

Eventually, he found a suitable boy named Abell Cooke. But this time, Master Giles had to draw up a formal apprenticeship agreement. Finally, the boy and his mother arrived at Blackfriars to sign the indenture. She was paid forty pounds for his services for a period of three years.

"Goodbye, dear Abell. Be a good boy for your master!" she bade him.

He looked after her sadly as she departed through the door with her pouch of gold crowns. He was a small boy with angelic looks. He had undoubtedly been picked to play the female roles. Master Kendall was delighted with his new acquisition. "He will be an asset to the company, Master Giles," he boasted.

"He has cost us a pretty penny," replied Master Giles dryly. "So let us hope that he will prove to be a worthy investment."

I looked at the newcomer avidly. The onerous duties of the dormitory would fall to the lot of the newest boy. His arrival was a benefit to the whole company, but especially to me. However, the austerity of our lives did not appeal to young Abell.

"I thought the life of a player would be jolly," he complained. "My mother said I would have good pastime and merry larks. But this is all work and no play."

As an apprentice he was allowed holidays to go home. But after only three months he left and never returned. His mother came and repaid the premium to Master Giles.

"He's not coming back no more and that's final," she sniffed. "He don't like it here."

Master Giles was furious that he had no power to retain him under the law. "It was much better to impress the boys, Master Kendall," he complained. "Then they knew that they must obey their masters. These apprentices grow saucy and discontented with their lot. And their families interfere with their training. Next time, we will buy a boy outright and there will be no more of this folly."

A month later he succeeded in buying a boy. There were plenty of poor families in London who were only too thankful to sell a child into a good trade. He had fine features, but his doublet and hose were threadbare and patched. He trembled as Master Giles paraded him triumphantly before Master Kendall.

"I paid eight pounds for him, Master Kendall," he announced with satisfaction. "His name is James Bristowe and he is nine years old. He will play the children's roles in the plays until he gets older."

"Well, he is fit to appear on the stage. But can he read, Master Giles?" he enquired doubtfully.

"He is illiterate as yet, but he will learn quick enough. One of the grammar school boys can teach him his letters and how to declaim. He must be ready to perform in three months."

"Very well," assented Master Kendall. I shall send Thomas to buy a hornbook. He will begin his lessons today."

The boy looked bewildered by the sudden change in his circumstances. He was given a set of livery to wear which was undoubtedly finer than anything he had worn before.

"You are now a member of a company of players, James," he informed him sternly. "My name is Master Kendall and I am your master. You will work hard and do everything that you are told to do. Is that understood?"

"Yes, Master Kendall," he promptly replied.

"You shall sit at this table and repeat your alphabet to Thomas. I will expect you to know your letters by this evening."

Young James Bristowe was fortunate to have the kindly Thomas as his teacher. But I still pitied him. We had been impressed to serve in the company, but we still had families. And when were grown to manhood we would regain our independence. However, his family had relinquished their rights to him and he was now the property of his masters. He had to obey them and please them in everything.

CHAPTER 2

Life at the Blackfriars Theatre

"Satan hath not a more speedie way, and fitter schoole to work and teach his desire, to bring men and women into his snare of concupiscence and filthie lustes of wicked whoredome, than those places, and playes, and theatres are"

(John Northbrooke, A Treatise wherein Vaine Playes are Reproved, 1577).

Master Giles was the choirmaster of the Chapel Royal and he instructed us in our art. "There are those who denounce the theatres and playhouses as sinks of sin. But for those who best understand the dramatic art, the stage is a harmless and innocent recreation; where the mind is recreated and delighted. Indeed, it is a school of good language and behaviour, that makes youth soonest man, and man soonest good and virtuous, by joining example to precept, and the pleasure of seeing to that of hearing. Its chief end is to render folly ridiculous, vice odious, and virtue and nobility so amiable and lovely that everyone should be delighted and enamoured with it. In short, it is an honourable calling to be an actor. From now on you are a company. You will work together like brothers. There will be no quarrels or sparring among you. No discord shall mar your unity!" We gazed back at him dubiously.

"Acting is a subtle art," he reminded us. "You are being trained to perform as masters of oratory and movement. You make your entrances with natural ease and address. Then you make your bow with the elegance of a courtier. You do not charge onto the stage like a stamping-stalking player that will raise a tempest with his tongue and thunder with his heels! On the stage you stand tall and you walk with grace. You do not slouch like peddlers! You conduct yourselves like young gentlemen and on no account do you stand fumbling with your buttons or clawing at your cods!"

And so, we were taught how to perform on the stage and many other things besides. We were instructed how to sing and we learned a repertoire of songs and choruses. We were taught how to dance as well as any courtier and to play merry tunes on the recorder and the lute. We learned how to juggle and to tumble in order to entertain the crowds. Above all, we were taught how to recite our speeches clearly and eloquently.

"No, no, boy!" he cried impatiently. "Not like that! Speak the speech as I pronounced it to you. The words should flow trippingly from your tongue. Don't bellow them out like the town crier on market day!"

Over time he introduced us to the finer points of performing on the stage: "An actor's performance adds grace to the poet's verse," he explained. "You must learn to employ the language of the hands so that the action is best suited to the word. The gesture must seem to arise naturally from the verse. When you are idle, you should fold your arms. When you are supplicating, you should stretch forth your arms. When you are disputing, you should clasp your hands. When are lamenting, you should wring your hands. The proper use of these speaking motions will enhance the power of your oratory. It is a form of manual rhetoric which will render your performance more impressive. The leading exponent of this art is Edward Alleyn of the Admiral's Men. He was the epitome of grace and charm upon the stage, but he has now retired from acting. Richard Burbage of the Lord Chamberlain's Men is now the most admired actor in London. He takes the leading dramatic role in every play and presents a most impressive figure on the stage."

I was disappointed to learn that I would never see Edward Alleyn perform. But I hoped that one day I would see the famous Richard Burbage and find out what made him so remarkable. Our training progressed to simple practice plays which we acted before our master's critical eyes. We had to become proficient before we could perform in front of an audience. Master Kendall conducted the rehearsals with the strictest discipline and had no tolerance for the slightest error. Our spirits wilted under his harsh regime and we began to dread the morning rehearsals. There was no appeal to Master Giles. He was equally severe and had regarded Master Evans as being too lax in his manner. The younger boys grew fearful and the older boys became resentful. The camaraderie we had once enjoyed seemed to evaporate and was replaced by an atmosphere of tension and apprehension. We practised diligently in order to meet the exacting standards of our masters. But we longed for the return of the genial spirit that had once infused our rehearsals.

Our next play was another comedy called "*Jack Juggler*." It told the story of the downfall of a lazy servant called Careaway. But this time I would be playing a female role instead of the male lead. I was cast as the maidservant Alice Trip-and-Go. Master Kendall took me to the tiring house and dressed me in a costume he had brought from his haberdashers' shop. It consisted of a gown and an apron, a pair of stockings and shoes and a linen cap.

"You must wear it all day to accustom yourself," he ordered. "Take care not to trip on your skirts. In time you will learn the proper management of them."

I picked up my skirts gingerly and tried not to catch my feet in the hem as I stepped onto the stage.

"You are not walking like a young girl, Nathan!" he scolded. "Put on this pair of chopines. They will make you step daintily."

I put on the heavy chopines, but I found they made it even more difficult for me to keep my balance. The other boys sniggered as they watched me mince my way around the stage and attempt to make a curtsey. We were filled with excitement at the prospect of turning our speeches into a comic drama. But it proved to be an entirely different experience from the pleasant rehearsals of "*Ralph Roister-Doister*." Our masters were very demanding and expected nothing less than perfection in mastering speeches, singing harmoniously as a chorus and playing an accompaniment on the lute and recorder. This arduous training was hardest for the apprentice boys. They lacked the experience in reading and declaiming of the grammar school boys and the musical skills of the choristers. Often their performance was less confident and polished and they suffered the consequences.

"*Jack Juggler*" began with a lengthy introduction about the importance of recreation and mirth. Philip Pykman had been chosen to deliver the Prologue. He was a former apprentice who was a strikingly handsome boy. But when he was only halfway through his speech, he stumbled and broke down.

Master Kendall was furious at such an ill beginning to our new endeavour. "You worthless lout!" he snapped. "I'll warrant you spent the evening playing at dice and cards instead of conning your lines!"

"I swear that I was not gambling, Master Kendall," he pleaded. His face was pale with fear.

"Nor playing at marbles or Nine Men's Morris I suppose?" he accused him. "Do you think what we do here is a game? Or that playgoers will come here to watch your mistakes? I will teach you not to tarnish the reputation of the company. You need to learn a lesson, you young rascal!"

"Please, Master Kendall!" he begged him. But it was to no avail. He was carried away under the strong arm of the stage manager to receive a sound whipping. Silence fell over the company as a series of pitiful shrieks pierced the air. Our sense of elation turned into gloom. *I won't let that happen to me,* I vowed to myself. *I will always know my lines and I will never be beaten!*

Philip was brought back in tears to continue his performance. Master Kendall brandished his birch rod menacingly. "Now begin again!" he ordered.

Philip stammered his way through his lines. Then it was our turn to speak. But we froze like statues upon the stage and delivered our lines with the gravity of a sermon. Master Giles pursed his lips and frowned disapprovingly.

Master Kendall glowered at us. "This play is a comedy! It requires lightness and ease. I can see that there is much more work required. Tomorrow we will rehearse in the morning and the afternoon. Now to bed with you all! Master Pykman, you will remain here!"

Philip was made to stand on the stage and recite the lines of the Prologue until he was word perfect. Only then was he allowed to go to the dormitory. He lay upon his pallet and sobbed bitterly. Some of the younger boys pitied him, but the older boys had no sympathy.

"When you make mistakes, it makes it worse for the rest of us!" said Robert sourly. "We have extra rehearsals tomorrow and it is all on account of you!"

"Leave him alone!" said Thomas with a frown. "He is a 'prentice boy, not a scholar or a chorister. I don't suppose he ever did much reading before now. Yet the masters expect him to have the same skills in declaiming."

"He will just have to apply himself harder to learn," retorted Robert. "Otherwise, it will be beaten into him with a rod."

Thomas sat down next to Philip's bed. "Take no notice of him," he said reassuringly. "Tomorrow you will know your lines and the masters will be content. A player must have audacity to please their audience. So, pluck up your courage!"

"I wish I was back in my 'prenticeship," he blubbered. "Master Chambers was a cobbler and he was kind to me. I always had enough to eat and he never beat me. I don't know why I was chosen to join a company of players."

"You have to forget about that now, Philip," he advised. "You are a player and you will soon adjust to the life of the stage. It's not such a bad life once you're used to it. But if you talk about your old master, they will think that you want to run away and they will punish you. You'll just have to make the best of it!"

Thomas was one of the kinder older boys. He set out to help the 'prentices for he saw that the masters lacked the patience to help them to learn. They were pathetically grateful and became devoted to him as their protector. Soon they were following him around like the Pied Piper. The other boys teased him and said that he was bound to end up as a schoolmaster. He did not seem to mind that the masters were imposing on his good nature. They did not pay him a penny for his labours.

For my part, I sought the friendship of the other grammar school boys, Jack Underwood and William Ostler. Our shared background created a bond between us. We could converse together in Latin which baffled the other boys. Nothing would have induced me to give up my precious time in teaching 'prentice boys how to read and declaim. I needed it for my own studies. It was their misfortune that they had ended up in this company, as it was mine. In my heart, I resented being taken away from my school. I had been a successful scholar with a bright future ahead of me. My family had been proud of me. But what kind of future did a player have?

The following day, we performed the play again. Much to our relief, Philip was able to recite his speech correctly. We settled down and performed our roles with greater confidence and animation. I made the most of the witty remarks of Alice Trip-and-Go. Jack played the role of my mistress, Dame Coy, and he responded with equal vigour. The scene came to life through our merry banter. Our enthusiasm was infectious and the other players joined in with equal abandon. Soon everyone was smiling and relishing the comedy.

"Why didn't you show such liveliness yesterday?" demanded Master Kendall. We stared down at the stage and made no reply. *He is no proper instructor of boys*, I thought. *He has no understanding and he thinks that admonishment is the key to success.*

Our next play was *"A pretty and merry new Interlude called The Disobedient Child."* It was a comedy which portrayed a wilful young man who married against his father's wishes and repented of his folly. The father lamented his son's reckless conduct:

"Nowe at the last I do my selfe consider
Howe great griefe it is and heviness,
To every man, that is a Father.
To suffre his childe to followe wantonnes."

The moral of the story was that children should be raised with strict discipline for their own good. It was not my idea of an entertainment, but I could see why Master Kendall liked it. I was cast as the shrewd Maid-Cook. And Philip was cast as the Prologue again, much to his dismay. But this time Thomas took him upstairs to the dormitory to practice. He trained him so thoroughly that by the time we retired we were all word perfect in it. The next day in rehearsal there were no mistakes in the speeches. I spoke my lines with the clarity of a herald angel, but I despised Master Kendall in my heart. The play ended with the players kneeling down on the stage to deliver an oration in praise of Queen Elizabeth:

"And last of all, to make an ende,
O God to the we most humblie praye:
That to Queene Elizabeth thou do sende
Thy lively pathe, and perfecte waye,

Graunte her in health to raigne.
With us many yeares most prosperouslie:
And after this life for to attaine,
The eternall blisse, joye, and felicitie.

And that we thy people duelie consideringe
The power of our Queene and great auctoritie,
Maye please thee and serve her without faininge,
Livinge in peace, rest, and tranquilitie.

God save the Queene."

This time the masters were satisfied with our performance. They turned their attention to teaching us to sing a set of madrigals. They were called *"The Triumphs of Oriana"* and had been composed in honour of the queen.

"Long live fair Oriana.
Hark, did you ever hear so sweet a singing?
They sing young love to waken;
The nymphs unto the woods their queen are bringing.
There was a note well taken.
O good, hark, how joyfully 'tis dittied;
A queen and song most excellently fitted.
I never heard a rarer, nor ever saw a fairer.
Then sing, ye shepherds and nymphs of Diana:
Long live fair Oriana."

"Fair Oriana, beauty's queen,
Tripped along the verdant green.
The fauns and satyrs, running out,
Skipped and danced round about.
Flora forsook her painted bowers,
And made a coronet of flowers.
Then sang the nymphs of chaste Diana:
Long live fair Oriana."

"You must sing these verses in a worthy manner," declared Master Giles. "One day you may appear before her Majesty at court."

I was amazed at the idea that one day we might go to a royal palace and entertain the queen. It seemed as glorious a notion as the vision of heaven in the Book of Revelation. At once I gained a higher impression of the lot of a player. I developed a burning ambition to excel as a performer so that I might be chosen to go to court. Surely that would make my family proud of my new livelihood!

As we became more proficient at performing roles, the masters gave out the parts to match our abilities. The former apprentices, Alvery

Trussell and Thomas Grymes, had less skill at reading and performing. They took the minor roles which had fewer lines to learn. The former choristers and scholars took the leading roles which had longer speeches. Salomon Pavy was tall and thin with straw-coloured hair. He was invariably cast as an old man and surprisingly convincing in the role. William Ostler had the loudest voice and played the role of the king. Jack Underwood had a turn for comedy and played the clown. Philip Pykman had plainly been selected for his good looks and he was cast in the female roles. It was the same in my case, but I played the queens and the heroines. I was determined to excel, so I did my best to copy the skills of the older boys. I had a good memory for learning lines and a pleasing voice for declaiming them. I had a natural affinity for the stage and enjoyed putting on costumes and playing different parts. I played the role of Dame Chat in "*Gammer Gurton's Needle*" and Lady Lucre in "*The Three Ladies of London.*"

A play was a new form of entertainment. The queen favoured showing plays at court because they were much cheaper to stage than a masque. Companies of actors were the latest novelty for the citizens of London. They enjoyed nothing more than watching a well-told story being acted in a tavern or one of the newly built public theatres. Since we were a children's company our masters selected comedies for us to perform rather than tragedies. The audience was charmed by the novelty of children playing adults, but the result was more effective when we performed amusing farces. Tragedies were better suited to adult companies.

Master Giles instructed us on the history of plays. "Dramatic plays first flourished amongst the Greeks, and afterwards amongst the Romans. They were almost wholly abolished when their Empire was first converted to Christianity, and the theatres and the temples were demolished as relics of paganism. Thereafter, only plays of the holy scriptures, or saints' lives were performed. There were no theatres or companies until the beginning of Queen Elizabeth's reign, when players began to assemble into companies, and set up theatres, first in the city and then in the suburbs."

Master Giles warmed to his theme. "There are three kinds of plays," he continued. "There are histories, comedies and tragedies. A tragic hero is characterised by *hamartia*, *hubris* and *nemesis*. In other words, they suffer from a fatal flaw. Their excessive pride leads to the vengeance of the gods. For example, the young Icarus foolishly failed to heed the warning of his father not to fly to close to the sun. Instead of keeping to the safe middle course, he rose ever higher in the sky. The wax in his wings melted and he plunged into the sea."

"Then his death was on his own head," I objected. "It was due to his folly, not the spite of the gods."

He glared at me. "We may say that his fatal flaw caused his downfall. His pride clouded his judgement and brought about his tragic death. The Greek writers were pagans, of course, but their beliefs echo the Christian teaching that your sins will find you out. The major dramatists of our time include Christopher Marlowe, Thomas Kyd and William Shakespeare. You will see examples of such tragic heroes and their fatal flaws in their plays. Tamburlaine the Great is the classic Aristotelian example of "a great man who made a mistake." He would like to conquer the world but is brought down by his excessive pride and ambition. Dr Faustus' ambitious quest for knowledge leads him to over-reach himself by selling his soul to the devil. In "*The Spanish Tragedy*," the noble Hieronimo sets out to gain justice for the murder of his son. But in his quest for vengeance, he loses everything. In each case we can see that the hero's own passions were the cause of their tragic fall."

From then on, Master Giles referred to me derisively as "*young Icarus*." I wished that I could play the role of one of these tragic heroes. But our company mainly played witty comedies where young boys could mimic adults to great effect. Our training was arduous and the days were long. It was not often that we were allowed a holiday. On those rare occasions we would roam the Bankside together in search of amusement.

"If only I had a penny I would buy some hot chestnuts," sighed Jack. He threw a pebble into the Thames and watched it splash.

"And I would buy a crusty meat pie," said Salomon. He was always hungry.

"Don't you know what goes into those pies?" asked William. "They are made from the hearts and livers of the felons executed at Tyburn."

"Liar!" I said. "There couldn't possibly be enough to fill all those pies."

"All the same, I wouldn't buy them," retorted William. "Let's go swimming in the river!"

"I can't swim," objected Salomon.

"Never mind!" I assured him. "We won't let you drown." Of course, we were strictly forbidden to swim in the river. But we always did. It was one of the few pleasures that we could enjoy for free. Sometimes we loitered around the marketplaces where we gazed enviously at the exotic goods on sale: the oranges, pomegranates, dates and figs. But the only fruit we ever enjoyed were apples stolen from orchards.

CHAPTER 3

The Court of the Faerie Queene

"O Goddesse heavenly bright,
Mirrour of grace and Majestie divine,
Great Lady of the greatest Isle, whose light
Like Phoebus lampe throughout the world doth shine,
Shed thy faire beames into my feeble eyne."

(The Faerie Queene by Edmund Spencer, 1596).

Finally, we were deemed ready to perform in public. The first play that our masters intended to present at Blackfriars theatre was *"Cynthia's Revels"* by Ben Jonson. I took the leading part of the queenly Cynthia. This time my costume was much more elaborate. It was a costly silk gown with a farthingale, petticoats and puffed sleeves. I wore silk stockings and a pair of spangled shoes. Around my neck was an elaborate starched ruff. An ornate fan with ivory sticks completed my ensemble. I felt that I could hardly move, let alone act in all this gear.

"It looks very well indeed!" declared Master Kendall with great satisfaction. "Your entrance should astound the audience. You must stand erect and walk with elegance like a great lady. And when you sit, you must convey a regal presence!" Fortunately, I did not have to perform a dance in this role. I did not think it would be possible in such ridiculous attire. My wig was made of real hair which was very expensive. It was kept on a stand in the tiring-house.

"You must take the greatest possible care of your costume!" Master Kendall admonished me. "It has been specially made at great expense. You must not get any marks upon it or you will be sorry!"

Naturally, the other boys teased me when they saw me all dressed up like the Queen of the May. But in time, I got used to wearing my flamboyant apparel. I even came to enjoy the attention that it drew from everyone who saw it. "*Cynthia's Revels*" was a well-written play and I enjoyed the humour of it. It was a clever satire on the court of Queen Elizabeth. Master Jonson guided us in the rehearsals and he was an excellent instructor. Master Kendall was pleased to have obtained the services of such a capable man. He had previously written his plays for the company of the King's Men until his latest work, "*Every Man Out of his Humour*," had proved a flop. When Master Jonson directed the rehearsals, it was quite a different experience for the company. "You may leave the boys to me, Master Kendall," he declared. "I have my own methods."

To my surprise, Master Kendall acquiesced to his demand. "Pay close attention to what he says," he told us. "He is better versed and knows more Greek and Latin than all the poets in England."

Master Jonson was the sort of person whom no-one tried to browbeat. He was a most imposing figure. His thickset frame and intense dark eyes commanded respect. His large nose and high forehead spoke of wisdom and experience. His brown hair and beard framed his face, adding to his gravitas. He wore a black doublet with a collar of starched white lace that marked him out as a man of authority. He was a temperamental man and jealous of his reputation. He was a veritable force of nature when he was aroused. But he showed nothing but kindness to the boy actors of our company. He began his rehearsals by telling us the story of the play. Soon he had us captivated. His pantomiming of the comic scenes made us laugh out loud. In our practice sessions he was demanding, but endlessly patient in achieving the results that he wanted. In return, we did everything we could to please him. He was an exceptional instructor who inspired the players onto new heights.

"Think about your roles, boys!" he urged us. "Don't confine yourselves to dead imitations of what you have done before. Act freely, carelessly and capriciously as if your veins ran with quicksilver. Your speeches should sparkle like salt in the fire!"

I was thrilled to be given permission to bring my own thoughts to my part. I envisaged Cynthia as a proud and noble queen. She was determined to amend the folly of the courtiers who surrounded her. My performance grew in confidence and authority.

Master Jonson encouraged me. "That's it, Nat! The queen should be a pattern of virtue in order to contrast with her dishonourable court. She should comport herself with grandeur and agreeable majesty!"

I blossomed under the influence of his great mind. He was tolerant of my questions and in time he became my good friend and mentor. Under his guidance I grew ever more adept as a player. I had a good voice and a natural turn for mimicry that stood me in good stead in comic parts. I had considerable self-confidence as a player and felt at home on the stage. It seemed quite natural that I should be cast in the leading role. The other masters began to hold me up for emulation to the other players.

"No, no, boy!" Master Kendall would say. "Watch how Nat does it!"

Even the austere Master Giles was impressed by my oratory. "Why can you not declaim it like Nat?" He has the proper sense of how to phrase it!" I began to feel proud of my calling as a player. It wasn't what I had chosen for myself, but it seemed as though I had a natural aptitude to succeed in the profession.

One day Master Jonson spotted me sitting at the table with my Latin primer. The other boys were engaged in playing a noisy game of forfeits. But I was determined to improve my learning as a scholar.

"What do you have there, Master Field?" he asked me.

I showed him my textbook. "We were halfway through Cicero's "*In Verrem*" when I was taken into the company," I told him. "But I want to continue my studies."

"A commendable aspiration, Nat," he replied. "Every player should be well versed in the classics."

Master Jonson had his own opinion of Master Kendall, as he did about everyone. "He knows nothing of literature and very little of plays!" he said dismissively. "He is a pure pedantic schoolmaster sweeping his living from the posteriors of little children." It was exactly my own opinion of him, only phrased much better. I considered Master Jonson to be the best wordsmith in London. I was glad to have found a capable teacher at last.

Our first public performance at Blackfriars theatre took place in December 1600. The play began with a comical scene of three players quarrelling over which one of them shall wear the black cloak and deliver the prologue.

Player One: "*You shall not speak the Prologue, Sir!*"
Player Two: "*Why, do you hope to speak it?*"
Player Three: "*I think I have most right to it: I am sure I studied it first.*"

Player One: "That's all one, if the Author think I can speak it better."

Player Two: "I plead Possession of the Cloak: Gentles, your suffrages I pray you."

The audience roared with laughter at the sight. Then it was my turn. I stepped onto the stage to give my first speech with my heart racing and my soul alight.

"When hath Diana, like an envious Wretch,
That glitters only to hjs soothed self,
Denying to the World the precious Use
Of hoarded Wealth, with-held her friendly Aid?
"Mortals can challenge not a Ray, by right,
"Yet do expect the whole of Cynthia's Light.
But if that Deities withdrew their Gifts
For humane Follies, what could Men deserve
But Death and Darkness? It behoves the High,
For their own sakes, to do things worthily."

In that moment I was no longer a boy from St Paul's grammar school. I was the goddess Diana presiding over my court of revellers. The assembled courtiers drank from the spring of Narcissus which made them become boastful and vain. A foolish courtier challenged all comers to a competition of courtly compliments, but lost. A group of dancers performed a masque in which vices masqueraded as virtues. I ordered the revellers to purify themselves by bathing in the spring of Mount Helicon. Finally, I spoke the closing words of the play:

"Now each one dry his weeping Eyes,
And to the Well of Knowledge haste;
Where purged of your Maladies,
You may of sweeter Waters taste,

And with refined Voice, report
The Grace of Cynthia, and her Court!"

The audience greatly enjoyed the play and it was judged a great success. I was congratulated on my convincing performance as Cynthia. Master Jonson was delighted and came to speak to me afterwards.

"You spoke the lines well for a boy of thirteen. Where did you go to school?" he asked me.

My heart raced as Master Jonson's eyes bore into mine. His praise was unexpected, yet it ignited a spark of pride within me. "I was a pupil at St Paul's grammar school," I replied, my voice steady despite the flutter in my chest. "I was sorry to leave off my studies so soon."

His imposing face softened, and he leaned in, as if sharing a secret. "I myself attended Westminster School and was compelled to leave in order to learn a trade. But I continued my studies on my own. There is no reason that you could not do the same." It was a new thought. It hung in the air between us like an invitation to reach out and grasp knowledge beyond the confining walls of the theatre.

"Do you really think so, Master Jonson?" I asked, my mind racing. In that moment the world opened wide before me. I wondered if I could continue my studies independently and gain the wisdom of a true scholar.

He saw my eagerness to learn and his eyes crinkled at the corners. "How far did you get with your Latin?"

Memories flooded back of my days at St Paul's school. I remembered the expertise with which Master Mulcaster had recited the texts to the scholars. His eloquence and passion had stirred something within me. "We translated parts of Livy's "*Annals of Rome*" and some of the speeches of Cicero."

"Then you have missed the best. The classical poets are the best models for aspiring writers. You should read the satires of Horace and the epigrams of Martial. It will help you to appreciate the plays in which you perform. I'll bring my books from home and we can read them together after the rehearsal. How does that sound?"

"I would be most grateful, Master Jonson." And so, I became his pupil. He had the greatest patience as a teacher and I was soon able to appreciate their beauty and wit for myself.

"Here are Martial's famous lines on *"The Good Life."* There is still much wisdom in them although they were written by an old Roman. I do not think there is anything I would add to his vision:

"These, my dearest Martialis, are
The things that bring a happy life:
Wealth left to you, not laboured for;
Rich land, an ever-glowing hearth;
No law, light business, and a quiet mind;
A healthy body, gentlemanly powers;
A wise simplicity, friends not unlike;
Good company, a table without art;
Nights carefree, yet no drunkenness;
A bed that's modest, true, and yet not cold;
Sleep that makes the hours of darkness brief:
The need to be yourself, and nothing more;
Not fearing your last day, not wishing it."

"I am not likely to have any wealth that is not laboured for," I said gloomily.

"Ah, that is but the start of his reflections, Nat. Riches, land and houses are the outward signs of wealth. But that is not sufficient for gaining lasting happiness. You will see that his conclusion is to find contentment within yourself. And that is the work of a lifetime. But here is another verse you should know. It is the first of his epigrams and merits special attention:

"Here's the one you read, and you demand,
Martial, who is known throughout the land
For these witty little books of epigrams:
To whom, wise reader, you keep giving,
While he still feels, among the living,
What few poets merit in their graves."

"It is a reminder to poets to seek not merely distinction, but lasting fame. The reward of genius is to gain immortality. But there are few writers today who can reach the great heights of Martial and Horace," he declared.

"Whom would you name, Master Jonson," I enquired.

"Well, I pass over myself, but if I were pressed to give a name it would have to be William Shakespeare. He is the star of poets and the playwright of the Globe theatre. His writing is not for an age but for all time." From then on it became my ambition to see the plays of Shakespeare on the stage. I hoped that one day I would act in them too.

"*Cynthia's Revels*" was performed several more times at Blackfriars theatre. As a company of child performers, we were considered a great novelty and the playgoers of London flocked to see us. As the weeks passed, we grew in confidence as performers. We knew our speeches perfectly and could give our full attention to perfecting the comic scenes and the musical interludes. But something we were not prepared for was the behaviour of the London gallants. It was their custom to rent a stool on the stage for sixpence in order to show off their grand clothes and feathered hats to the other playgoers. They would invariably take their places at the very last moment and interrupt the Prologue. Then they would smoke tobacco and play cards with their friends throughout the first act. But they were not content to leave it there. They would laugh aloud in the middle of the tragic scenes and deliberately spoil the mood of the drama. The most outrageous of the gallants would compete with the players for the attention of the audience. They would mock our costumes, whistle at our songs and interrupt our speeches with sarcastic remarks:

"They look like little wrens hopping about on the stage! Their singing is vile enough to stretch a man's ears worse than the pillory! And their stench would poison me if it was not for my tobacco!"

Their jeering threw us off our performance and made us nervous. It only encouraged them to behave even worse. Nothing delighted them more than to disrupt the play entirely and make it a failure. They would stand up in the middle of the performance and cry: "A vile piece! I can tolerate no more!" Then they would leave the theatre with all their friends and hope to persuade the rest of the audience to follow them.

But Master Jonson had their measure and explained how we should retaliate. "Unfortunately, hecklers are the plague of every theatre. You cannot allow them to get the better of you and undermine your confidence. Instead, you must find a way to discomfort them in front of their friends. Once you prick their pride they will shrivel up and slink away. I give you my leave to abuse them to the best of your ability!"

We soon became the terror of the gallants. We strove to outdo one other in the extravagance of our insults: "Your wit is as thick as a Tewkesbury mustard! More of your conversation would infect my brain." "Your face would sour ripe grapes!" "You are as loathsome as a toad; I am sick when I look at you!" And if anybody walked out of the performance we would call after him in chorus: "A pox go with you!" It added to the entertainment of the crowd and enhanced our reputation for witty comedy. Jack Underwood was the most fearless of us all and excelled in his inventiveness. When one foolish gallant persistently interrupted his speech, he kicked over his stool and stood over him in triumph. "You are a base, proud, shallow, beggarly, three-suited, hundred-pound, filthy, worsted-stocking knave!" he declared. The audience roared with laughter and the braggart was so humiliated that he was forced to crawl away into the wings. He never returned to trouble us again.

The success of *"Cynthia's Revels"* made our name as a company. Master Kendall informed us that we had been honoured with an invitation to perform the play at court. We would appear before the queen on Twelfth Night which marked the end of the Christmas celebrations. And so, on the morning of 6th January 1601 we travelled by barge along the freezing river Thames to Hampton Court Palace in Richmond. Each of us carried our costumes in a bag. Hampton Court was a magnificent pleasure palace made of pink bricks with a great paved courtyard. It had once been the residence of Cardinal Wolsey, but it had come into the possession of King Henry VIII. When we arrived, we were conducted to the Great Hall which had a splendid hammerbeam roof and a set of huge tapestries displayed upon the walls showing scenes from the life of Abraham. At the far end of the hall, a stage had been set up with crimson velvet curtains and a painted backdrop. A profusion of wax candles had been strung across the hall on wires to provide sufficient light for the performance. We changed into our costumes and took our places for the Prologue. I felt nervous about performing the part of a queen before her Majesty, Queen Elizabeth.

There was a fanfare of trumpets as the queen made her entrance. All of us made a deep reverence to her. She was dressed in a magnificent gown of white silk, bordered with pearls the size of beans. Over it she wore a mantle of black silk shot with silver threads. Around her neck she wore a great gold collar set with jewels. Her train was very long and was carried by her chief lady in waiting. She sat on her chair of estate beneath a canopy of crimson velvet. Her ladies stood on each side of her with the maids of honour behind them. They wore white gowns and were all very beautiful. Master Kendall announced *"A performance of Cynthia's Revels, or the Fountain of Self-Love. A new comical satire by Master Ben Jonson. As performed by the Children of the Queen's Revels."*

When I stepped out onto the stage dressed in my regal costume, I heard the whispered voices of the court ladies raised in admiration:

"Did you ever see a prettier child? See how he behaves himself and speaks and looks and holds up his head? Bless his little heart!"

Master Jonson had included a masque scene to appeal to the queen's taste. Four nymphs and four elves stepped onto the stage. The nymphs wore gowns of yellow and green and the elves wore costumes of green and blue. They partnered each other in a series of enchanting dances. The queen's ladies broke out into cries of delight. The play was interspersed with songs in praise of the queen. I could see that she enjoyed these compliments for she smiled and nodded.

> *"Queen, and Huntress, chaste and fair,*
> *Now the Sun is laid to sleep,*
> *Seated in thy Silver Chair,*
> *State in wonted manner keep:*
> *Hesperus entreats thy Light,*
> *Goddess excellently bright.*
>
> *Earth, let not thy envious Shade*
> *Dare itself to interpose;*

*Cynthia's shining Orb was made
Heaven to clear, when Day did close:
Bless us then with wished Sight,
Goddess excellently bright.*

*Lay thy Bow of Pearl apart,
And thy Crystal shining Quiver;
Give unto the flying Hart
Space to breath, how short soever:
Thou that mak'st a Day of Night,
Goddess excellently bright."*

After the performance, the queen withdrew to her apartments attended by her ladies. But the young maids of honour hovered around to pet us and make much of us. They said that we looked and sang like angels. We revelled in their admiration for our tutors rarely praised us. Even at our young age we were sternly admonished to conduct ourselves like men. Sir Edmund Tilney, the Master of the Revels, brought Master Kendall his payment for the performance. Finally, he beckoned to us to withdraw. Immediately we formed ourselves into an orderly procession to make our departure from the Great Hall. Just then a page boy dressed in the royal livery brought him a message.

"Her Majesty wishes to see the boy who played Cynthia," he announced. All eyes turned to me. Master Kendall drew himself up with pride.

"He will be honoured to see her Majesty," he replied. "I will bring him myself."

"Just the boy," said the page. "Come with me, sirrah." I was still dressed in my majestic gown, but I followed him through the door that led to the queen's private apartments. It was guarded by two tall Yeomen of the Guard holding their gilt battle-axes. They were clothed in scarlet tunics embroidered with gold roses. A sudden anxiety seized me. *What if I have offended her Majesty?* I thought. *Maybe she thinks that I am mocking her in my queenly gown?* My heart plummeted at the fearful prospect and I wished that Master Jonson was with me. He would defend his players and his play even in the face of a wrathful queen.

"Her Majesty will receive you in the Paradise Chamber," he said. "It is a great honour. Only the foreign ambassadors are invited to see her here." We walked through a chamber with a gilded ceiling which shone like a vision of heaven. Its walls were hung with costly hangings of blue, green and yellow silk embroidered with strange birds and beasts. I stared at them in astonishment. I knew the other boys would never believe me when I told them what I had seen.

"They come from the land of China far to the east," he informed me. "They were a gift to the queen from the earl of Essex." It was common knowledge that Essex was the queen's favourite courtier.

On the other side of the chamber was the queen's "Paradise Room." It was aptly named for it had a beautiful painted ceiling and its walls were decorated with hangings of green velvet sewn with gold trees and flowers. On the window sills were displayed seven long cushions of cloth of gold and cloth of silver. The floor was spread with rich Turkey carpets where the ladies in waiting sat upon large floor cushions. There was a cupboard the breadth of the chamber which stood six stories high. It was full of sumptuous gilt plate and on the topmost level was plate of pure gold to furnish the queen's table.

Another tall cupboard housed the queen's book collection bound in red leather and blue velvet. On a table lay a set of virginals made of mother of pearl and a lute tied with green ribbands ready for the queen's pleasure. Silver-gilt plates set with burning candles hung upon the walls to give light in the chamber and a great fire burned in the fireplace to make it warm. On the mantle stood a cunningly wrought clock in the shape of an Ethiopian riding upon a rhinoceros. Above it hung a needlework map of Britain and a map of the New World drawn in coloured ink. In the midst of the chamber sat the queen under a gold canopy covered with jewels. She smiled at me benevolently as I approached her. I was filled with relief to see that her Majesty was not looking displeased. I could not bow in my gown, so I made a deep curtsey to her instead.

"So here is the little queen," she remarked as I stood before her. "What is your name, young man?"

"I am called Nathan Field, your Majesty," I replied. At such close quarters I could see the true splendour of her dress and jewellery. In her ears she had two rich pearl earrings. On her head she wore a red wig that was similar to my own and a gold coronet. Her face had been painted into an impenetrable mask of white, but her dark eyes were shrewd and searching.

"A perfect little courtier!" she remarked. "But would you rather serve us as a pageboy or a maid of honour?"

"Whatever shall please your Majesty the best," I replied, making another curtsey.

Her lips twitched. "Bravo! It is a true courtier's answer!" she said. "For such a reply, you may have my hand to kiss."

She drew off her long silk glove and extended her right hand towards me. It was sparkling with rings and jewels. I saluted it and made a third curtsey to her.

"I see that your master has taught you proper courtly manners. Does he allow you to eat comfits, Master Field," she asked me with a smile.

I shook my head for we were strictly forbidden to eat sweetmeats. "No, your Majesty," I said.

"Today you shall, for you deserve a reward," she declared firmly. She gestured to her lady in waiting who picked up a small box and brought it over to me.

"These are the queen's favourites," she informed me as she placed it in my hands.

"Thank you, your Majesty," I exclaimed in delight. My heart swelled with pride at the knowledge that my performance had pleased the queen and her ladies. How foolish I had been to worry! I vowed never to doubt myself again. I made a final curtsey and retreated from the queen's presence without turning my back on her. I wondered what was inside the box and when I would have an opportunity to open it. I knew that I must keep it out of Master Kendall's sight at all costs or he would confiscate it. Then I would never know what sort of comfits it contained.

The page conducted me back to Great Hall where Master Kendall and the company were waiting impatiently. "What did her Majesty say to you?" he demanded.

I thought quickly. I could not say that the queen wanted to give me a reward. It would betray my secret. And he would be sure to feel slighted. "She sent you her compliments upon our training and performance, Master Kendall."

His frown subsided and his countenance lightened. "Indeed? That is most gratifying to hear. Well, you must hurry to change out of your costume or else we shall miss the tide."

I concealed the queen's gift in my costume bag on my way back to Blackfriars. When we returned to the dormitory, I hid it under my pillow. The other boys clamoured to know what I had seen in the queen's apartments.

"I was taken through a chamber which was hung with golden silks from China. Then I was brought into the Paradise Chamber where the queen sat upon a great throne. There were mirrors on the walls with lights of wax as big as torches. There was gold and silver everywhere you looked. She had a great cupboard full of gold plate which was worth a king's ransom and another cupboard full of dozens and dozens of books, more books than you have seen in your life" I replied. I wished that I had had a chance to look at the queen's wonderful library.

"What did she really say to you? I don't believe she sent Master Kendall her compliments!" said Jack.

But even my friends could not know the truth. I did not want the older boys to seize my prize from me. "She said that she was pleased to see such bold children perform in her palace and she would send for us again."

The boys were pleased and fell to discussing their impressions of the day. They were particularly impressed by the magnificence of the Great Hall. My mind kept turning to the contents of the box. I wondered again what dainties were inside it. In the middle of the night, I finally felt it was safe to look at my present. When I opened it, a delicious scent filled the air. The box was full of sugared violets. I made short work of the queen's comfits, but I kept the box to show to my mother. I recited my speeches and sang the songs from the play for her benefit and I boasted of the queen's favour to me. Afterwards, I always thought fondly of the queen. She was my first patron and giver of largesse. I learned that there were special rewards to be gained from being a good performer. I looked forward to receiving more of them.

CHAPTER 4

The Boy Actor

*"There is, sir, an aery of children, little eyases,
that cry out on the top of question, and are most
tyrannically clapped for't: these are now the fashion"*

(Hamlet Act 2, Scene 2)

The following month there was a great stir in the city. The queen's favourite courtier, the earl of Essex, had been sent to Ireland to fight against the rebels, but instead of defeating them in battle he had agreed a truce. The queen was furious at the news and upon his return to England he had been sent from court in disgrace. On the morning of 7th February 1601, a finely dressed gentleman came to Blackfriars to call upon Master Kendall.

"I am Sir Gelly Merrick and I have a commission for your company of players."

"How can we serve you, Sir Merrick?" replied Master Kendall eagerly.

"It is his lordship, the earl of Essex, whom you may serve. He wishes you to stage a special performance of a play called "*Richard II.*""

"It is an old play, Sir Merrick. But I have a copy of it. When would his lordship like it to be performed?" he asked.

"Today, Master Kendall," he answered.

"But the company must have some time for rehearsals!" he protested. "Today is quite impossible!"

"The players may hold their prompt books in their hands," he said. "'Tis no matter as long as their lines are clearly spoken." He pulled out a fat leather purse and handed it to Master Kendall. "His lordship will pay you forty shillings. Will that content you?"

Master Kendall took the purse and bowed. "I am entirely at his lordship's service. I shall prepare the play at once and I assure you that he will be entirely satisfied."

"I expected no less of you, Master Kendall. I shall inform his lordship of your good service." He swept out of the door. Immediately, Master Kendall told the clerk to draw up a playbill and paste it onto the door. Then he summoned the company to the hall and allocated the roles to the players. I was cast in the role of the tragic king.

"We shall begin the rehearsal at once," he ordered. "We will be performing the play this afternoon."

Somehow, we managed to present the play creditably. Sir Merrick and a group of his friends took their seats on the front row and watched the performance intently. During the abdication scene he called out, "Yea! And so, all weak kings should fall!" As the crowds of playgoers departed from the playhouse, he congratulated Master Kendall on a most stirring performance. The following morning the earl of Essex, his supporters and two hundred soldiers gathered at Essex House. They took to the streets calling upon the citizens of London to rally to his defence and march upon Westminster. However, his quarrel was none of theirs and nobody took any heed. The earl and his followers were arrested and taken to the Tower. After the commotion was over and order was restored in the city, Master Kendall received a visit from Sir Henry Carey, the Lord Chamberlain.

"How was it that you came to perform that particular play in public on the day before the rebellion?" he asked severely. "Didn't you realise that it was intended to stir up the people into feelings of indignation against her gracious Majesty?"

Master Kendall turned pale with fear. "We had no notion of what was intended, my lord. We were commissioned to perform that play for his lordship's pleasure and so we presented it."

"You should have sought my advice before taking such a course, Master Kendall. You are either a blockhead or a traitor! These rogues wanted to sway the minds of the people to their cause and bring events from the stage to the state!"

"I assure you that the entire company are quite devoted to her Majesty. They are desolate at having been practised upon in this manner, my lord."

"Her Majesty wishes to see this play for herself. You will bring your company to court on the morrow and present it to her." He turned and stalked away leaving Master Kendall full of apprehension. He sent for Master Giles to come post-haste. Then he sat at the table with his head in his hands. Finally, Master Giles arrived looking perturbed.

"A terrible thing has happened, Master Giles," he exclaimed. "I don't know what is to become of us. I performed *Richard II* as I was requested. But now I am suspected of treason. I have been ordered to take the boys tomorrow to perform before the queen. But I fear I cannot do it. I am quite unmanned with dread. I beg you to take the company to court in my place!"

I could see from Master Giles' expression that he had no intention of going to court. "It is you they wish to see, Master Kendall," he replied unsympathetically. "Pull yourself together. This is no time to lose your nerve. Do you want to appear like a guilty man?"

He sat up and wiped his eyes. "I am sorry, Master Giles. But it is enough to dismay anyone."

"Did you not think it was a strange choice of play?" he admonished him.

"Indeed, I thought it most odd that the earl would request to see and old play rather than a new one. But who can tell what whims a great lord may have? It was not my place to question him, Master Giles."

"That is all you need to say to her Majesty and her councillors," he advised. "You can hardly be blamed for performing an old play. As far as I can recall, it expresses nothing treasonable."

"That is true, that is true," he said pathetically.

"Take my advice and bring her Majesty a gift when you attend court tomorrow. And don't fret about it. This matter will all blow over, Master Kendall."

The following day, Master Kendall was more himself as he ushered us down to the river Thames to take the barge to Whitehall Palace. It was the most impressive of all the queen's residences. Every part of it demonstrated splendour and luxury worthy of the tales of the Arabian Nights. It had been built to express the power and wealth of the English court and its monarchy. I felt proud that as one of the Children of the Chapel Royal, I was a servant of the queen with the privilege of serving in her royal palaces. We traversed the shield gallery which was hung with hundreds of paste-board shields from the queen's tilt-days. Then we passed through the Privy Chamber with the great mural of King Henry VIII and Queen Jane Seymour. He stood with his feet placed apart looking the very image of majesty. The imposing figure of the king struck awe into the hearts of all onlookers. We continued into the Presence Chamber with its ornate gilded ceiling and splendid tapestries. Finally, we arrived at the Great Hall where we were due to perform. At the end of the Great Hall a temporary stage had been erected. We put on our gaudy costumes and took our places for the first scene.

The queen looked most imposing as she entered the hall and took her chair of estate. She was dressed in a splendid gown of white satin embroidered with gold. She had great ropes of pearls draped around her neck and she looked every inch a monarch. The Lord Chamberlain and the entire Privy Council were there in attendance. The expressions on their faces were as grim as if they were presiding at a trial. As before, I took the title role of King Richard II in the play. Finally, we reached the abdication scene. I hardly dared to look at the queen as I recited the ominous words:

> "Now mark me, how I will undo myself;
> I give this heavy weight from off my head
> And this unwieldy sceptre from my hand,
> The pride of kingly sway from out my heart;
> With mine own tears I wash away my balm,
> With mine own hands I give away my crown,
> With mine own tongue deny my sacred state."

Queen Elizabeth sat there looking inscrutable under her white makeup. But by the time the performance had ended, she had relaxed into a smile. She had clearly decided that there was nothing provocative in the text or the action of the play. I stepped forward and presented her with a bouquet of red silk roses. She smiled and accepted them graciously.

"So, the little queen has become a king, I see," she remarked. "Really Lord Carey, this play is quite harmless. I enjoyed seeing the performance. But I prefer something more light-hearted." She rose majestically and left the hall followed by her ladies. The Lord Chamberlain informed Master Kendall that the queen and her privy councillors had concluded that he had been a dupe of the conspirators and had no knowledge of their plot. He was cleared of any suspicion of treason.

The following day, the earl of Essex and four of his followers were executed for high treason. We were sternly forbidden to discuss the matter, but in the marketplaces the citizens avidly discussed the latest rumours. Some held that the earl had intended to put down the Privy Council and replace the queen's advisers with his own supporters. But others firmly believed that his purpose was to seize the crown and make himself the king. In any case, he was considered to be a most ambitious and dangerous man. The story of his rise and fall would have made a marvellous plot for a tragedy. There is no doubt that the playgoers would have flocked to see it. But there was no way that the censor would every have permitted such a such a play to be performed in public.

The earl of Southampton was imprisoned in the Tower for his part in the rebellion. The gossip of London claimed that his pet cat had missed him so much that it had made its way to his cell by climbing down the chimney. But the boys in my dormitory dismissed it as a tall tale. I wished that I had a cat of my own. One day I found a stray cat wandering alone on the Bankside. He was black and white with a fine set of whiskers, but as thin as a rail. I knew that he would not survive much longer living outside in the cold. So, I brought him back and hid him in the dormitory. At once the other boys gathered around and argued over what we should call him.

"How about Tamburlaine the Great?" proposed Jack enthusiastically.

"Too long," said Saloman. "He would end up being Tam."

"We could call him Grimalkin!" suggested William.

"No, he's a black cat. Let's call him Hades," said Saloman.

"I like the name Merlin," I insisted. "Look, he's got a beard like a wizard!"

The cat, oblivious to our discussion, blinked at us with amber eyes. He was quite content to live in our dormitory. He spent his nights sleeping on our pallets and his days sitting on the windowsill staring out at the patchwork of rooftops that surrounded us. Master Kendall was surprisingly tolerant of the company owning a pet cat. He thought that he would bring us good luck. So, he named him Felix and he became a regular playgoer and a firm favourite with the crowds.

The queen showed that she harboured no ill-will towards our company by inviting us to return to court the following month and perform another play. This time we presented a blameless old production called *The Contention between Love and Prodigality.*" It was a comedy in which Prodigality declared that the princely heart that freely spends gains friends, praise and love. Vanity wondered how it was that folk continued to follow fortune as though it were a thing of certainty. But Virtue asserted that no ease, no pleasure, can be good, that is not got with pains.

> *"Though Virtue's ways be very strait,*
> *Her rocks be hard to climb:*
> *Yet such as do aspire thereto,*
> *Enjoy all joys in time.*

This therefore is the difference,
The passage first seems hard
To Virtue's train; but then most sweet
At length is their reward.

To those again, that follow vice,
The way is fair and plain;
But fading pleasures in the end
Are bought with lasting pain."

The queen and her ladies seemed to enjoy it immensely. Queen Elizabeth had a reputation for being careful with money, so the subject was much to her taste. I concluded our performance by giving a loyal speech to her Majesty.

"Most mighty queen, yonder I sat in place,
Presenting show of chiefest dignity;
Here prostrate, lo, before your princely grace
I show myself, such as I ought to be,
Your humble vassal, subject to your will,
With fear and love your grace to reverence still."

In the summer of 1601, the queen and her retinue departed on a progress of Hampshire to visit her courtiers at their great houses of Cowdray, Basing, Elvetham and Farnham Castle. The royal party rode on horses to allow the queen to be seen by her subjects. A great baggage train of two hundred carts travelled ahead carrying their goods and supplies. I was fascinated at the thought of it. I had never been out of London. There would be presentations in the towns along the way. There would be masques and banquets in the great houses. I would have liked to go and see these wonderful things!

Shortly afterwards, my wish was granted. Master Kendall announced that we would be travelling north to give a performance at a house in Derbyshire.

"Why are we going there?" asked Saloman in astonishment.

"The Queen has commanded it," replied Master Kendall sternly. "It is a great honour. We are to entertain the household of a great lady who is a close friend of her Majesty. Her name is Lady Elizabeth of Shrewsbury and she lives at Hardwick Hall."

"What shall we give them? Will it be *"Cynthia's Revels"*?" said William.

"Aye, and then *"The Spanish Tragedy."* And there is a good comedy called *"The Gentleman Usher"* that I think they will like."

It seemed that we were back in favour again at court. Our progress was much humbler in nature for we only had four carts. But the journey into Derbyshire was fraught with difficulties. Even though it was August, the weather was inclement and the roads were bad. The wardrobe master fretted over the state of his precious costumes. The players grumbled about the poor food and hard beds at the country inns. Finally, after ten days we arrived at Hardwick Hall. Never shall I forget the sight! The hall was a newly-built residence as fine as a palace. It towered above us and its tall glass windows glinted in the pale sunlight. The initials "ES" dominated the parapet.

"Elizabeth of Shrewsbury" muttered Master Kendall.

Our carts pulled into the stable courtyard and we prepared to disembark. Immediately, the head groom appeared and challenged us.

"I don't know any of you. And you're certainly not from around here. Who sent you?"

Master Kendall drew himself up proudly. "Her Majesty sent us to perform for your lady. We are the Children of the Chapel Royal."

The head groom pursed his lips and shook his head. "You can't come in here. These are the stables for the gentry. You are to stay at the old hall until my lady sends for you."

Lady Elizabeth owned two houses at Hardwick. There was the new hall which housed members of the family and their honoured guests. And there was the old hall of red bricks which housed the servants and the less distinguished visitors. We turned the carts around and guided them into the old stable yard. The grooms took care of our weary horses and the housekeeper took us to a long table in the great hall. We were served with bowls of hot potage, trenchers of bread and cheese and jugs of small ale. Afterwards she led us to a large dormitory lined with pallets up in the attics. But it was comfortable enough after our days on the road. We were just settling down for a much-needed rest when a page dressed in blue livery brought an urgent message.

"Lady Elizabeth has been informed of your arrival. She wishes to see a performance this evening. It is her intention to see as many plays as possible during your visit."

Master Kendall was taken aback. "The stage has not been assembled nor have the costumes been unpacked. My players are too exhausted from the journey to perform today. Tell her ladyship that we will be pleased to entertain her tomorrow night."

The page looked shocked by such a response. "Tell my lady what will happen in her own house!" he exclaimed. "If she says that she will see a play, then you will perform! You had better hurry to put up the stage. I will show you the way to the Reception Chamber."

Much to our surprise, this chamber was not on the ground floor of the house. Instead, it was located on the upper floor. We gazed at the massive oak staircase with awe and dismay. Master Kendall turned to the house steward who was hovering over us with a disapproving look.

"We can't possibly set up our stage upstairs. Your staff will have to take it up there."

"The servants are busy with their own duties. Your men look sturdy enough to me."

Master Kendall pursed his lips. "We'll have to perform without the staging. We've done it before."

And so, we hauled our heavy boxes of props up the steep flights of stairs from landing to landing until we reached the upper level. I had to admit that the Reception Chamber was a magnificent setting for a performance. The tall glass windows revealed a view of the formal garden laid out below. Displayed on the window sills were seven long cushions of cloth of gold, cloth of silver and white satin embroidered with silver. The walls were hung with a series of tapestries depicting the story of Ulysses. Above them ran a plaster frieze with painted scenes from the Hardwick estate. The royal arms of Queen Elizabeth I were prominently displayed above the chimneypiece. They comprised the figures of a lion and a dragon and the motto: "*Dieu et mon Droit*." No-one could doubt Lady Elizabeth's loyalty to the crown.

We hung up the curtains at the back of the chamber, arranged the costumes on their wooden stands and lit dozens of candles. Then we held a quick rehearsal while the household dined. Afterwards, they processed into the reception chamber and took their seats. Lady Elizabeth sat right at the front on a high-backed chair of needlework with a gold and silk fringe. She was dressed in a gown of black velvet with a starched linen ruff and heavy gold chains. Next to her sat a pretty young lady who wore an elaborate gown set with costly spangles. I stared at them in fascination until Jack dug me in the ribs.

"The old lady is the wealthiest woman in the kingdom. She has been married four times."

"She can't have been," I objected.

"That's why she's so rich," he remarked, as he adjusted his lace collar. "She was first married at the age of twelve. It's what the gentry do."

"Who is the young lady next to her?" I asked. She stood out in the midst of the company as a vision of youth and beauty. Her jewelled gown sparkled in the candlelight as a testament to her wealth and status. She was clearly someone of great importance.

"That is her niece, Arbella Stuart," he replied. His voice dropped to a low whisper. "She is a cousin of the Queen. In fact, she may be the next queen one day."

"How come you know so much?" I demanded.

Jack grinned and his eyes gleamed with merriment. "I was talking to one of the housemaids over at the old hall. The servants here are proud to work for such a grand family. You need to start using your noddle, Nat. There are opportunities in performing in places like this. The old lady never comes to court or sees any entertainments. So put on a good show this evening!"

That first night we performed *"Cynthia's Revels"* which we knew they would not yet have seen. At the end of the play, the old lady nodded approvingly. But Lady Arbella was entranced. Her gloved hands applauded us with enthusiasm.

"It is wonderful, grandmother!" she declared. "How I wish I could go to court and see more of these performances!"

"You must be patient, my dear," admonished Lady Elizabeth. "The queen has shown us great favour by sending her players to entertain us. You must be sure to write to her and thank her for her kindness. Tomorrow you will see another play."

"What will it be, grandmother," she asked breathlessly.

"That will be a surprise. And now it is late so we must retire." Lady Elizabeth rose and swept out of the chamber followed by her granddaughter and their ladies.

The second night we played *"The Spanish Tragedy"* and the third night we performed *"The Gentleman Usher."* Finally, our visit to Hardwick Hall was concluded. We waited expectantly for our reward. The house steward walked over to Master Kendall and handed him a leather purse.

"My lady was pleased by your performances," he informed him. "She has given you this present."

He smiled and gave a gracious bow. "I am most grateful to her ladyship," he replied.

He walked behind the stage curtain and opened the purse. We looked on eagerly. The purse contained twenty shillings. His face fell. After all our efforts, it was only a shilling for each of us. Clearly, we were not going to make our fortunes here. Later that night in the attic of the old hall he complained about her miserliness.

"That is why she is so rich!" he grumbled. "She grudges to spend her coin too freely. The queen is far more liberal. She always pays ten pounds for every performance! This is the last time that I ever will make a tour in the provinces. There is no profit to be found in it!"

The journey back home to Blackfriars was equally damp and uncomfortable. But we enlivened our tedium by discussing the servant's gossip about the great family whom they served.

"Do you really think that one day that young girl will be the next queen?" I wondered.

"Well, the housemaid was convinced of it," replied Jack. "She thinks that she is going to serve her young mistress in a royal palace in London."

"Nonsense!" snapped Master Kendall. "Those servants are deluding themselves with their silly dreams of grandeur. Anyone who does not know that the next heir will come from the line of Scotland is a fool!"

"What about the old lady then?" said Jack. "She is as rich and imperious as the queen herself. The family already behave as though they were royalty. Look at how grandly they live!"

Master Kendall was still smarting over his petty reward. "She may be great in Derbyshire, but that does not make her a power at the court. The Privy Councillors will be the ones to choose the next successor, you mark my words!"

In February 1602 we were summoned to appear before the queen at Whitehall Palace again. We had prepared a new play called *"Poetaster"* by Ben Jonson. It was a satirical comedy set in ancient Rome. I was cast in the role of Augustus Caesar who regarded poetry as the most perfect of the sciences. I passed judgement upon the poets of my day. I honoured Virgil and Horace but punished the inferior poets Crispinus and Demetrius. Master Kendall was certain that it would amuse the queen. She was known to have received a classical education and would surely appreciate the erudite jokes. The whole company looked forward to playing before the queen again. The play began with a complimentary Prologue addressed to her Majesty:

> "Our eyes are dazzled by Eliza's beams,
> See (if at least thou dare see) where she sits.
> This is the great pantheon of our goddess,
> And all those faces which thine eyes thought stars,
> Are nymphs attending on her deity."

But on this occasion the queen looked older and wearier. She did not take the same interest in our performance as she had before. Her ladies appeared anxious and subdued. There was no sense of excitement surrounding our performance. Our confidence began to falter and our singing fell out of tune. Afterwards, the Master of the Revels, Sir Edmund Tilney, rebuked Master Kendall.

"I thought I told you to present something new and diverting for her Majesty. But this was poor stuff. It was stale and tedious. It is no wonder that she was bored."

"A thousand apologies, Sir Edmund," he stammered. "I assure you that our next performance will be everything her Majesty desires."

"You will be informed if her Majesty wishes to see you again," he replied loftily.

Master Kendall was disappointed. He blamed us for failing to entertain the queen. "It is an excellent script and very much to her Majesty's taste. If you had been livelier and more comical in your performance, then it could not have failed to please her."

Our hearts were in our boots. We had looked forward to performing at the court. We could not think what had gone wrong. Only Jack had the courage to protest. "It was not our fault, Master Kendall. The queen was falling asleep almost as soon as she took her chair."

Master Kendall glared at him. "It is a poor excuse to blame the audience. It is your task to win them over and charm them by using your art. The patronage of the queen means everything. The reputation and future of the company depends upon it. Today you have failed to please the court. It must never happen again!"

But later that evening I heard him in earnest conversation with Master

Giles. "I fear that her Majesty is now too old to take any pleasure from an entertainment."

His eyebrows drew together in perturbation. "That cannot be the case. Her Majesty has always enjoyed seeing new plays performed at the court. Our livelihood depends upon it!"

"What will we do if she does not send for us again?" lamented Master Kendall.

"The court must keep up appearances regardless of her Majesty's inclinations," insisted Master Giles. "The Master of the Revels must provide a series of festivities to celebrate Christmas and Easter. There are still foreign dignitaries to be entertained. Depend upon it, he will invite us back again."

"He blamed me for bringing a feeble play to court. Yet, everyone has praised it as an excellent comedy!"

"He is not going to admit that her Majesty is failing. She must still appear as the youthful virgin queen. We should commission a piece which will flatter her vanity. Something that proclaims loyalty and affection for the queen, but with plenty of humour. Tell Master Jonson to write some poetic speeches and merry songs. I will devise a pleasing story around them. We cannot afford any more mistakes!"

The play was to be called: "*The Loyal Subject*." But before it was half completed the queen had died. Master Jonson immediately focussed his attention upon penning speeches of welcome and praise for the new monarch, King James I.

CHAPTER 5

The Accession of King James I (1603)

"The wisest fool in Christendom"

(The Court and Character of King James I, Sir Anthony Weldon, 1650).

"The king hee hawkes, and hunts,
The lords they gather coyne;
The judges doe as they weere wont;
The lawyers they purloyne.
The clergie lyes a dyeing;
The commons toll the Bell;
The Scots get all by lyeing;
And this is England's knell"

(Popular verse)

After the death of Queen Elizabeth in March 1603 the theatres were closed as a sign of respect. No-one could talk of anything but the question of the succession. Some thought that it would be her Scottish cousin, King James. Others believed that it would be her English cousin, Lady Arbella Stuart. Everyone feared that a civil war would break out or else there would be an invasion from Spain. The citizens of London were relieved when Lord Robert Cecil read out a proclamation in Cheapside which named her successor as King James IV of Scotland and I of England. There would be no question about the succession in the future for he was married to Queen Anna of Denmark and they had three children named Prince Henry, Princess Elizabeth and Prince Charles. He was only too pleased to be chosen as the new king and set out at once from Holyrood Palace in Edinburgh on the long journey down to London. He sent word to the Privy Council to proceed with the funeral of Queen Elizabeth without delay. It was said that he did not wish to honour the dead queen because she had ordered the execution of his mother Mary, Queen of Scots.

As a consequence of the succession, we boys had a holiday from rehearsals. It meant that we were free to roam around London. At the end of April 1603, we stood in the crowds to watch the old queen's cortege pass by on its way from Whitehall Palace to Westminster Abbey. There was a great procession of mourners dressed in black. First came two hundred and sixty poor women in new mourning gowns and the queen's choristers singing dolefully. Then came the aldermen and the Mayor of London, the Privy Councillors, the bishops and the nobility of the kingdom. The queen's hearse was draped in black velvet and pulled by four horses. As it passed by, the crowds groaned and wept with sorrow at the sight. Behind the coffin walked the queen's ladies in waiting and maids of honour. The queen's guards brought up the rear carrying their halberds downwards. A young apprentice standing next to us informed us that an old lion named Elizabeth which had been kept in the Tower had pined away with grief after the queen's death. She had reigned for forty-four years. Everyone wondered what the new reign would bring.

King James arrived in London at the beginning of May and many of the prisoners in the Tower were released to celebrate. They included the young earl of Southampton who had taken part in the late rebellion. We looked forward to the pageants which would take place to celebrate the coronation at the end of July. However, there was an outbreak of the plague that summer and the ceremonial procession through the streets of London had to be postponed. People were disappointed not to see the new king. Master Jonson had written a welcoming address in praise of the new king and queen for one of the city pageants and had rehearsed me in it most diligently. He was sorely vexed when his flattering speech had to be delayed. He was keen to make a good impression upon the new monarchs. I went to visit my mother at Grub Street. She was glad to see me but urged me to forsake the vain life of a player.

"Your brother Theophilus believes that it is the playhouses which are bringing down the wrath of God upon us. He thinks you should turn away from this sinful life and settle to some useful trade. Then you could marry and raise a family like any other God-fearing man."

I refused to believe that the plague was divine retribution. And I was disappointed that my mother saw no merit in my work as a player. "Many of the Puritans think that the plague is a sign of God's displeasure at a Scottish monarch on the English throne. It is just as nonsensical a notion."

She clutched a worn Bible to her chest. "You should not repeat such idle gossip, Nat. It could be regarded as treason!"

"I am sure that you will not denounce me, mother," I replied impatiently.

"All the same, you should be more careful," she said in a hushed voice. "Players are held in suspicion by the authorities and there are spies everywhere."

"It is Theophilus who will have to be careful," I answered defiantly. "I doubt that the new king will be as tolerant of the Puritan preachers as the old queen was."

"Why do you say that Nat?" she asked in dismay.

"Didn't Theophilus tell you latest news from court? When the Puritans spoke against ceremonies because they had been used when England was Catholic, King James said that shoes had been worn when England was Catholic, so why didn't the Puritans go barefoot?"

My mother had failed to convince me to change my way of life, so one day my brother Theophilus paid me a visit. He had achieved considerable success in his career in the church. I could understand that I was an embarrassment to him.

"I only want what is best for you, Nat," he insisted. "As your older brother I am responsible for your welfare. The life of a player is unnatural. You spend your days in make-believe and your nights at the tavern. And the Bankside is the worst place in London. It is a nest of gambling dens, brothels and cutpurses. You are still a young man and your life will be corrupted. Why waste your God-given talents as a player on the stage?"

I was irritated by his criticisms. He had never been to Blackfriars and was merely repeating the common prejudice against playhouses and players. It was often said that a Puritan was a man who loved God with all his soul, but hated his neighbour with all his heart.

"I will tell you Theophilus," I retorted. "As an actor I bring pleasure and laughter into people's lives. And as a playwright I open up their minds and encourage them to think about the world."

"Pleasure is an empty bubble," he replied disapprovingly. "I have been told of these plays and their themes are immoral. The playgoers come only to enjoy the spectacle of violence, horror and depravity."

"The playgoers can take whatever message they choose from the plays. I am not there to preach to them. But they can see that evil leads to tragic consequences."

He shook his head and got up to leave. "One day you will come to see that this is all vanity, Nat. I stand ready to help you whenever you need it. I shall keep you constantly in my prayers until then."

"Farewell, Theophilus," I said. I knew that he meant well, but it vexed me that he could see no merit in my chosen profession. The Puritans were constantly lobbying for the closure of the playhouses. They regarded them as a threat to public morality. It made the life of an actor even more precarious.

A new drama arose to occupy the attention of the citizens of London, for not everyone was pleased to welcome the new king. He had brought a host of Scottish favourites to England and appointed them as his Gentlemen of the Bedchamber. Sir Robert Cecil kept his post as the Lord Treasurer, for he was irreplaceable. But Sir Walter Raleigh was forced to resign his role as the Captain of the Guard. A number of other courtiers of Queen Elizabeth I also lost their positions under the new regime. It created an atmosphere of discontent which overshadowed the start of the new reign.

Not long afterwards, Raleigh was accused of conspiring with Thomas Grey, Henry Brooke and George Brooke to depose King James and replace him with Lady Arbella Stuart. They were arrested and taken to the Tower of London. The news of the plot caused a sensation in London. The citizens wondered if the new reign would begin in bloodshed and muttered that it would be an ill-omen. Master Jonson was troubled for

Raleigh was a patron of writers and a notable poet. He took me along to attend the trial. Henry Brooke had made a confession which named Raleigh as one of the conspirators. But there was no other proof against him. Raleigh put up a spirited defence of himself.

"Let me confront my accuser face to face," he demanded. "This is a matter of life and death, not a dispute over a small copyhold!"

But the tribunal refused to call Henry Brooke to testify and be cross-examined. Raleigh maintained his innocence of the whole affair.

"How could I be in the pay of Spain?" he declared. "I am Spain's greatest enemy and all the world knows it!"

But his protests were all in vain. He was found guilty of treason and sentenced to death. However, he was still a popular figure. People remembered his victories against the Spanish Armada and at Cadiz. So, his sentence was commuted to life imprisonment in the Tower. Master Jonson was deeply grieved at his friend's plight. He regarded his downfall as an injustice against one of the nation's greatest men.

"Only a tyrant would cage such a bird!" he muttered; his voice barely audible.

"He was one of Queen Elizabeth's favourite courtiers," I interjected softly. "King James could have made good use of his talents."

Master Jonson's eyes flickered. "Talents!" he scoffed. "Raleigh had too many powerful enemies at court. They feared his influence and contrived to bring him down. What a waste of a fine man!" I nodded, understanding the forces that had been aligned against him. His victories had elevated him, but they had also made him the target of envy. His downfall had been orchestrated by those who resented his brilliance.

"Now he will be remembered as a traitor instead of a hero," I remarked sadly. "No-one will dare to speak up on his behalf. He will end his days as a prisoner in the Tower." It was a common enough story. But common folk like us could do nothing about the intrigues of the court. It was the price which ambitious men often had to pay for their success.

Master Jonson straightened, determination sparkling in his eyes. "There is still the power of the pen, Nat," he declared. "The stage is a formidable device. I shall lay his case before the public." I looked at him doubtfully. The censor would object and he risked offending the king. But his resolve was unyielding.

"I shall disguise it as an historical tragedy," he assured me. "But the message will be quite apparent to those who have the ears to hear and the wit to understand!"

Master Jonson duly began his new play called *"The Tragedy of Sejanus."* He intended it to be seen as a protest against the times. Sejanus was the head of the Praetorian Guard and the favourite of the Roman emperor Tiberius. But at the height of his power, he was denounced by his enemies and executed without a trial. As the play took shape I wondered: *Could the stage truly sway hearts? Could it resurrect a fallen hero?* Master Jonson meant to draw a parallel between the treason trials and the repression of Tiberian Rome. His description of the emperor portrayed him as a tyrant:

> "Dead to virtue, he permits himself
> Be carried like a pitcher by the ears,
> To every act of vice: this is a case
> Deserves our fear, and doth presage the nigh
> And close approach of blood and tyranny."

I thought it was very bold of Master Jonson to speak up for his friend. However, all the theatres in London were closed. He could not present his play to the public until the plague had subsided. He chafed at the delay for his feared that his topical allusions would lose their effect. However, the new king and queen were not prepared to forgo the customary Christmas entertainments. In order to commemorate the start of a new reign, the planned festivities at Hampton Court were particularly splendid. No less than thirty plays would be performed before the court including a production of *"Robin Goodfellow."*

In December 1603 our company was brought to the palace to prepare for a special performance. We were required to take in a new masque for Twelfth Night called *"The Vision of the Twelve Goddesses."* We would rehearse under the direction of Sir Edmund Tilney, the Master of the Revels. I was delighted to be taking part in the first court masque for the new king and queen. The writer of the masque was a playwright named Samuel Daniel. He was an elderly man who had been a court poet to Queen Elizabeth I. He was present at the first rehearsal to give us our instructions.

"The queen has commissioned me to write this masque," he announced proudly. "It is one in which she takes a personal interest for it will celebrate the peace and unity of the reign of King James. Indeed, she and her ladies intend to appear in it. You shall be the actors who provide the words for the masque. It is a great honour for you. You will be performing before the king and the greatest nobles in the land."

"But won't the queen and her ladies want to give their own speeches?" I enquired.

"No, no, it would be beneath their dignity," he assured me. "Noble men and women may dance in public, but they do not act upon the stage like common players. So, the queen and her ladies will enliven the court with their dances and the actors will present the speeches to the audience."

"The queen herself will dance?" I asked incredulously.

"Yes, that is what she says. It will prove an astonishment to the court, that is certain!"

We returned to Blackfriars chattering as excitedly as a flock of starlings. On our next visit to the palace, the costumes were provided for the rehearsal. They had been taken from the wardrobe of the late Queen Elizabeth and remade into fantastic attire for the performers. There was a buzz of excitement as we tried them on. They were embroidered with gold thread and adorned with gold spangles. We had never worn anything so costly before. "These buttons are made of solid gold," Jack whispered to me. "They would be worth a mint at the pawnbrokers!"

Sir Edmund Tilney eyed us with disapproval. He was as pompous and fussy as ever. "You boys must take the greatest care of these costumes. Each one is a priceless work of art. Not a single spangle must be lost or you will smart for it!"

Master Kendall was most put out by the insinuation. "I assure you, Sir Edmund, that all the boys of the Chapel Royal are honest subjects of their Majesties!"

"No doubt, Master Kendall," he replied, looking sceptical. "But I am accountable for the good condition of these costumes. Any damage or loss will be punished most severely."

Master Kendall drew himself up to his full height. "There is no question of anything going missing," he retorted. "You may take my word for it!"

Sir Edmund Tilney raised his eyebrows. "I hope so for your sake, Master Kendall. In the reign of King Henry VIII a pageboy was caught snipping off the ornaments from the gown of his mistress. He was hanged as a thief!" After this exchange there was no love lost between him and Master Kendall.

When Master Jonson heard the news about the masque, he was at first incredulous and then furious. He had no doubt that he had the greater talent, yet he had been overlooked. He made us recite our speeches to him after every rehearsal. And then he grilled us on the details of the production: What was the device and the allegory? What manner of scenery and costumes were planned? What music and dances were being prepared? Finally, he was satisfied that the intended masque was in every way inferior to what he would have devised in his place.

"Pah! It is mere froth and air with no substance whatsoever to it!" he muttered in disgust.

The presentation of the queen's masque marked the climax of the Christmas celebrations. *"The Vision of the Twelve Goddesses"* took place at nine o'clock in the evening. The courtiers and ladies filed into the Great Hall and took their places. All of them wore their most splendid and costly dresses for the occasion. When the company were assembled, the doors of the Great Hall were flung open, and the heralds proclaimed the arrival of the king. A fanfare of trumpets sounded and the whole company arose to make their obeisance. He sat beneath the canopy of state, placed near the beautiful south oriel window. The Great Hall was a magnificent sight. It was lit by hundreds of candles hung upon wires. The gold embroidered wall tapestries glittered in the light. An artificial mountain had been constructed at the far end of the hall. At the opposite end, on the left-hand side, stood the Temple of Peace. I played the role of Iris, the messenger of the gods, wearing a gown which was striped with all the colours of the rainbow. I announced the descent of the goddesses from Mount Olympus:

> "I, the daughter of Wonder, am here descended, to signify the coming of a celestial presence of goddesses, determined to visit this fair Temple of Peace, which holy hands and devout desires, have dedicated to unity and concord."

The ladies of the court descended from the mountain in groups of three. The queen led the way playing the part of Pallas Athena. She was followed by her favourite ladies. Lady Bedford played the part of Vesta and Lady Rich played Venus. They wore mantles and petticoats of different colours which had been taken from the old queen's wardrobe. Queen Anna was the most splendid of them all. She wore a blue mantle embroidered in silver and a helmet set with jewels. Each of the ladies was followed by a torchbearer dressed in white with gold stars. When the goddesses reached the foot of the mountain, they walked down the centre of the Hall to the Temple of Peace. They presented their gifts at the temple, while the Three Graces stood upon the dais, and sang the song *"Reward."*

> *"Desert, Reward, and Gratitude,*
> *The Graces of Society,*
> *Do here with hand in hand conclude*
> *The blessed chain of Amity."*

At the end of the song, the goddesses danced their measures with great majesty and art, finally forming themselves into a circle. Twelve lords came forward and partnered with them to dance in a lively set of galliards and corantoes. Then I returned to announce the departure of the goddesses. They performed a short parting dance and then retired up the mountain again. By then it was midnight and the company departed to partake in a banquet.

It was a memorable evening and I thought the spectacle was quite breathtaking. The only fly in the ointment was Master Jonson. He sat with his friend, Sir John Roe, guffawing throughout the whole performance. The honourable company turned around and glared at their irreverent merriment. But it only served to make them more boisterous. Finally, the duke of Suffolk stalked over to their chairs. He had a severe expression on his face and his hand was resting on his dagger. "Out!" he said shortly. Master Jonson and his friend were forced to make a hasty exit from the court.

But the following day he repaired to the Mermaid tavern and cheerfully recounted his exploits to his friends. He spent the next hour ruthlessly denigrating his rival over a bottle of canary wine.

"Why did their Majesties ask him, of all people?" he demanded. "Daniel is no poet! My cat could compose better verse! He is a mere scrivener with no more imagination than a gnat. A simple technician and no artist! A masque of Twelve Goddesses indeed!"

"What do you think he has planned for his next masque," I asked mischievously.

"You may well ask, Nat! I shudder to think of it!"

"We should put our heads together and compose *"The Masque of the Mermaid"* as a tribute to him," I proposed.

"You have hit upon it, Nat!" he roared and slapped his knee with pure glee. "Yes, indeed. Our worthy tavern keeper shall play the part of Neptune and his beauteous barmaids shall process before him in the guise of mermaids and pay him their homage. In the meantime, I shall deliver the speech of honour."

Sir John Roe nudged him. "There may be spies watching you, Ben!" he warned him. But there was no stopping him. He called over the tavern keeper and barmaids and explained what he wanted them to do. They were willing to oblige Master Jonson's fancy for a while. However, their enjoyment palled long before he had tired of the novelty. We were all thrown out of the tavern.

"'Tis no matter," announced Master Jonson. His good humour was fully restored. "The beer is far better at the Mitre. We shall take our custom there instead."

But as the evening drew on, he turned despondent and maudlin. The neglect of the court had wounded him. "Never try to make your living as a writer, Nat. It has beggared me. If I had taken up another profession then I might have been a rich lawyer, physician or merchant instead."

"Why do you do it then, Master Jonson?" I asked.

"I am compelled to do it," he said regretfully. "We all have a destiny and this is mine. My inner spirit drives me on to win fame and recognition from an indifferent world. I would that it was not so!"

"Then the world would have lost a great writer and philosopher," I replied stoutly.

He sighed gustily. "Our court is rife with corrupt place-seekers like a larder full of rats! It seems to me that there should be someone bold enough to contest the errors of our time. But writing satire is like walking along a knife edge. You can fall and cut yourself to pieces at any moment. I have already gone to prison for drawing attention to iniquities. It was a necessary price!"

CHAPTER 6

The Jacobean Court

"It is proper to say that not only the arms but also the speech of women should never be made public"

(Francesco Barbaro, On Wifely Duties, 1416).

The procession of the king and queen through the city of London was rescheduled for 15th March 1604. The Mayor of London sent out his orders for the traditional welcome to be prepared. Festive archways and platforms were erected across the city for the performers to present their speeches and songs. At daybreak our company were taken by cart to Cheapside. We changed into our costumes and Master Kendall rehearsed us yet again in our performance. Already the crowds were being to gather in the streets and the squares.

"It must be louder or else they will not be heard over the noise of the crowds," insisted Master Jonson.

At midday the Mayor of London and his company of aldermen arrived dressed in their scarlet costumes. By then the crowds were ten people thick. We took our places on the platform under the triumphal archway. We were costumed as angels of peace in tunic and hose of white satin with gold sashes. The women exclaimed at the sight of us.

"The pretty dears! Lord love them!"

Finally, we heard the sound of cheering and the carriage bearing the king and queen arrived and halted in front of us. They were dressed in royal robes of red velvet furred with white ermine. King James had brown eyes, a long nose and a pale complexion. His hair and beard were light brown. Queen Anna had blue eyes and a fair skin. Her abundant auburn hair was dressed with pearls and she wore a double rope of pearls around her neck. She looked around and smiled very affably at the crowds, but the king looked straight ahead of him. The expression on his face was proud and stern. "Now, Nat!" hissed Master Jonson. I stepped forward and gave my speech of welcome:

"Your Gracious Majesty,
I tender thee the heartiest welcome, yet
That ever King had to his Empires seat:
Never came man, more long'd for, more desir'd:
And being come, more reverenc'd, lov'd, admir'd:
Heare, and record it: 'In a Prince it is
'No little vertue, to know who are his.
With like devotions, doe I stoope t'embrace
This springing glory of thy god-like race;
His Countries wonder, hope, love, joy and pride:
How well doth hee become the royall side
Of this erected, and broad spreading Tree,
Under whose shade, may Britaine ever be."

I was aware of the king's dark eyes gazing at me intently. The rest of the company struck up their song of loyalty and then performed a graceful dance. The crowd applauded our pageant with great enthusiasm. Afterwards, the Mayor of London made his speech to the king and queen and presented the king with a velvet purse full of gold. But even that did not make him smile, although he thanked him gravely. The bestowal of the city's gift should have concluded the ceremonies at Cheapside. But the king beckoned me to come over to him. I hastened over to his carriage and made my bow. He looked me up and down.

"He is a bonny young lad, is he not my dear?" he remarked to the queen.

"Indeed, he is a very proper child, well-spoken and clothed like an angel of gladness," she agreed.

"Who taught you those words, boy?" he asked.

"They were written by Master Jonson, your Majesty," I replied.

"Why I know the man," exclaimed the queen. "He wrote the "*Masque of Satyrs*" which was presented before me at Althorpe House last June. It was a splendid performance. I spoke of it to your Majesty when we met the next day at Easton Neston."

"We shall see one of these masques performed at court," said the king. "And perhaps this pretty young fellow will entertain us again."

"I should be glad to do so, your Majesty," I said with alacrity.

"Whose company do you belong to, my boy?" he enquired.

"We are called "*The Children of the Revels*," your Majesty," I replied.

"I shall become their patron, your Majesty," said the queen. "From now on they shall be known as "*The Children of the Queen's Revels*.""

"It is a good notion, my dear," he observed. "They are a set of fine manly boys, right enough. We shall send them an invitation to come to the palace and they shall show us more of their dancing and singing. But now we must away or we shall be late for the banquet at Westminster."

I bowed again as the carriage pulled away. Women cried out, "God bless the good queen!" But people murmured about the new king's haughtiness after his carriage had gone past. "He's not as gracious to us as the old queen," they complained.

Soon afterwards, Master Kendall received official notice that the queen wished to become our patron. He was delighted by this sign of royal favour. At Easter 1604 the plague finally subsided and the theatres reopened again. We received an invitation to come to court and perform a play before the king and queen. Master Giles rehearsed us in "*The Tragedy of Sejanus*" and it was presented before the court at Whitehall Palace. I wondered if King James would take offence at the subject, but it seemed that the trials of the previous year had already been forgotten. Queen Anna and her ladies were quite delighted with us.

"Such charming little boys! How well they can play and sing! And how delightfully they speak!"

Queen Anna had the same love of splendid clothes and costly jewellery as Queen Elizabeth. She did not have the same stately manner, but she was a very pleasant and affable lady. And King James was far more affable in his palace than he was in public.

"So here are our angels come to visit us at court! It is a pleasure to see them again! I recognise the young fellow who made such a fair speech at Cheapside. Come here, young man!"

I stepped forward and made my bow. He ruffled my hair and tweaked my ear playfully. "He has a fine figure and a golden voice. One day he will be a prince of players if I am any judge of such matters."

"Your Majesty is too kind," I replied.

"*Arma virumque cano, Troiae qui primus ab oris Italiam, fato profugus, Laviniaque venit Litora"*. Did you understand what I said?" he asked, leaning forward with a smile.

I recognised it as the opening lines of Virgil's *"Aeneid."* "Yes, your Majesty," I replied promptly. *"I sing of arms and the man, who first from the shores of Troy, exiled by fate, came to Italy and the Lavinian shores."*

"I see you are well-lettered. But d'ye ken how to ride and bring down a deer with a crossbow, hey?" he demanded.

"I have never ridden a horse nor have I been on a hunt, your Majesty," I confessed.

"More's the pity for you'd have made a fine young squire," he said regretfully. "Take this, my boy." He gave me a ring from his hand.

"I am greatly honoured, your Majesty," I said in astonishment.

"It is a token of my regard," he said, patting my arm. "You have the bearing and manner of a nobleman's son. 'Tis unfortunate that you should have been born a commoner. But the stage is a good place for you to display your talents to the world."

I was cock-a-hoop at the favour the king had showed me. But Master Giles seemed displeased. When we returned to Blackfriars, he scolded me for posturing on the stage.

"Next time we go to court, do not be so quick to put yourself forward."

"But the king summoned me!" I protested.

"Do not contradict me, boy. It is pert and unbecoming," he snapped.

I put it down to jealousy on his part. But when I showed my ring to Master Jonson, he scowled and shook his head with foreboding.

"Beware of the favour of kings, Nat!" he warned.

"What do you mean, Master Jonson," I asked.

"For one thing, their favour is fickle. And for another, it provokes envy. Take my advice and put that ring away."

I was mystified by Master Jonson's disapproval. It was Jack Underwood who enlightened me. "The king doesn't have any mistresses at his court. He prefers the company of handsome young men instead. If you had been better born, he might have chosen you as one of his favourites. Then you could have made your fortune from him."

We performed at the court many more times. But the king never sent for me again. Evidently, my lack of gentility was distasteful to him. However, Queen Anna took great pride in being our patroness and revelled in our artistry. Her eyes glowed with approval and she always complimented us warmly on our performances. She paid Master Giles handsomely every time he brought us to court. A company of boy actors was considered a great novelty and we never failed to impress the ambassadors and foreign visitors.

Later that year, the King's Men came to Blackfriars theatre to perform the tragedy of "*Othello*." Naturally, all the boy actors were eager to see the play. We were given leave to stand at the back of the hall and warned not to disturb the paying customers. I stood there with Jack and William, eager for the drama to begin. At the last minute, Master Jonson arrived and took a seat hear the back of the hall. The play caused a sensation. Richard Burbage was outstanding in the role of the tragic hero Othello. He took three curtain calls from the audience. After the performance, Master Kendall persuaded Master Burbage to speak to us and he graciously agreed.

"People call us vagabonds, but we are artists," he declared. "On the stage our words have power over the emotions of men. We can make them laugh and cry as we please. We can enable them to forget their troubles for an hour or two. We can hold them spellbound with our storytelling and transport them to other world by our oratory. Indeed, we can create whole new realms of the imagination. We are paid little more than common labourers but we follow a noble calling. On the stage a poor beggar boy can become a prince if he has the talent and the application to master his craft."

"But who gives you the words, Dick?" interjected one of the other players. "The finest actor in the world would be dumb and powerless without the inspiration of the playwright."

"And the greatest playwright in the world would be nothing but a poor, unknown scribbler without the skill and passion of the actors to put life into his words, Will" he retorted sharply.

"Then let us agree that both these talents are mutually dependent," he said agreeably and wandered away into the wings.

"He will have it that he is the sole maker of our fame and prosperity, but it is my name that the audience shouts at the curtain call!" muttered Master Burbage.

Master Shakespeare was one of the leading actors in the company and had a rising reputation as a playwright. Our company had performed his *Henry VI* in which I had played Queen Margaret of Anjou.

"Does anyone have any questions for Master Burbage?" asked Master Kendall.

I stood up as I had been taught. "Very well, Master Field," he concurred.

"Why did Iago betray Othello?" I asked.

"Is it not enough to say that he was born wicked?" he replied.

"He had no good reason to do it," I persisted.

"Quite so. It is a fair question. A player must always understand his character. It could be that just as Othello was jealous of his wife, so Iago was jealous of his captain. Or that he harboured a grudge for failing to promote him. Or that he suspected him of seducing his wife. Or else he was in love with the fair Desdemona himself and destroyed what he could not possess."

"Then it would have been better for him to murder Othello and contrive to marry his widow," I objected.

"I see that you have a taste for revenge tragedies," he observed. "Indeed, they have become quite the vogue in the playhouses. But such an ending would show vice rewarded instead of virtue. It would not meet with the approval of the Lord Chamberlain. A little ambiguity can leave room for different interpretations. While it is necessary to give the audience a satisfying ending, it can be useful to leave them wanting to know a little more. Then they will walk away pondering the play in their minds and remember it for longer."

"Thank you, Master Burbage," said Master Kendall. "We will not detain you further."

Afterwards, we repaired to a tavern. My mind was still whirling from the power of the dramatic speeches and the tragic climax. We took a table and ordered tankards of small beer all round. Then we discussed our impressions with great enthusiasm. Othello was clearly a tragic hero with a fatal flaw. He was an honourable soldier who was undone by his jealousy. But Master Jonson was strangely silent.

"What did you think of the play?" I asked him.

"It was well enough. Indeed, a well-crafted tragedy. But I have a greater liking for a subtle comedy." Master Jonson regarded himself as the king of comedy writers.

"Do you have such a play in mind, Master Jonson?" I enquired.

"Perhaps," he said thoughtfully. "It is a new idea and there is no rush to complete it."

After watching *"Othello,"* I was keen to see other plays by the King's Men. They performed at the Globe which was the largest and most successful theatre in London. I persuaded Master Jonson to take me there to a performance of Hamlet. It was only a penny to stand in the yard. The Globe was an outdoor theatre located in Southwark and it could hold up to three thousand people. When we entered the side-gate that led inside, I was staggered by the sight. Above the yard were three levels of galleries where the audience could sit on benches to watch the performance. The heaving crowds in front of the stage were making a tremendous racket. Master Jonson pushed his way through them impatiently and found us a place with a good view. The backdrop of the stage depicted the scene of a painted castle. Two large thrones stood upon the stage for the king and queen. A player dressed in a black cloak stepped forward and announced *"The Tragedy of Prince Hamlet of Denmark"* as performed by Master Richard Burbage. The crowd gave a great cheer.

A fanfare of trumpets announced the entrance of the royal couple on the stage. A boy actor played the part of Queen Gertrude. I burned with envy as I watched him recite his speeches. I knew that I could play the part much better. When the ghost of the dead king appeared on the rampart, the crowd fell silent. He wore full armour, with the visor raised to reveal his face and silver beard. Master Jonson gave my arm a nip. "That's Will Shakespeare," he whispered. "He's the playwright." The ghost urged Prince Hamlet to take revenge for his death. The prince engaged a troupe of players to enact a murder before the king and queen. The king recoiled from the sight and stalked off the stage. Throughout the play, Dick Burbage held the crowds entranced as Hamlet struggled to keep his vow of revenge.

> *"What a piece of work is man! In the grand theatre of existence, we emerge—fragile and fierce, curious and contemplative. Our minds, like constellations, weave stories across time and space. We ponder the heavens, unravel secrets, and dance upon the precipice of understanding."*

The play was a long one with five acts. Between the scenes, young women wandered the pit with baskets of gingerbread and sweetmeats crying "Sweet china oranges, only sixpence each." Ballad mongers added to the clamour as they brandished their scripts and bawled out the latest ditty. Pickpockets preyed upon the crowd and were soundly trounced if they were detected. In the final act of the play a trap drop opened and a comic gravedigger appeared. I laughed when I saw his grizzled head suddenly pop up from below.

Master Jonson nudged me in the ribs. "It's Robert Armin," he hissed in my ear. "He always plays the clowns."

The play ended tragically with the death of the king, queen and Hamlet. Then the players came forward to take their bows. The audience whistled and applauded Burbage loudly. The crowds then dispersed in the fading light. "Let's get a hot pie," said Master Jonson. There were plenty of hawkers waiting outside the doors of the theatre. We bit into our pastries hungrily.

"So which part would you play, young Nat?" he asked me.

"The queen," I replied.

"Why not Orphelia?" he enquired.

I shook my head. "I'd rather be the queen. She pretended to be honourable, but she was guilty all along. I'd like to play her death scene."

He laughed. "And what did you think of Dick Burbage?"

"He is the king of players," I declared. "I'd like to play a scene with him."

"Perhaps you will one day. The theatre is a small world. There are only about two hundred people in it. Players and writers, managers and stagehands. You will come to know most of them before long."

Master Jonson advised me to visit the Mermaid tavern on Bread Street in Cheapside. All the players and writers of note were known to gather there and converse about the latest ideas. And so, I did, but I was too shy to join in their conversations. I was conscious that I was only a boy player and I knew nothing of court gossip or news from abroad. I feared that they would laugh at my presumption. However, one day I made the acquaintance of a young law student called Francis Beaumont. He was a handsome young man dressed in the style of a London gallant. He was sitting on a stool at a table in the Mermaid tavern. A scattered set of pages lay in front of him. I would not have dared to approach him, but he was an avid playgoer and he recognised me.

"I've seen you before, I think," he said, with his eyes narrowed. "On the stage at Blackfriars. You played the lead in *Cynthia's Revels*.""

"Master Field, at your service," I replied politely. I could see from his fine dress that he was a gentleman's son. He was only a few years older than myself with a handsome face and curly black hair.

He inclined his head. "Master Beaumont," he replied. "I am a student of the law at the Inns of Court. But I prefer to spend my time in writing verse. Alas, my muse has deserted me today. I have not completed a single couplet that is to my liking. But where are my manners? Sit down here and join me. Perhaps you will be able to give me some inspiration."

We spent the rest of the afternoon in conversation and we finished the verse between us. Afterwards, it became my regular custom to drop into the Mermaid after the morning rehearsals and discuss poetry and literature with Master Beaumont. He was fascinated with the world of the theatre and confided to me that it was his intention to write a play one day. I had nothing but admiration for his ambition. Master Beaumont was not one to let the grass grow under his feet. He realised that he needed the advice of other playwrights. He had the confidence and the means to cultivate the acquaintance of John Fletcher. One afternoon, I came to the Mermaid to find them engaged in a lively discussion of the tragedy of "*Sejanus.*" Master Beaumont quickly introduced me to his new friend.

"This is Master Field who is the leading player of "*The Children of the Queen's Revels.*" He has played in several of these historical plays."

"These ancient tragedies are falling behind the times," Master Fletcher declared impatiently. He was about the same age as Master Beaumont, but he dressed neatly rather than flamboyantly. "What people really want to see is a modern comedy of manners. Not something set in a royal court or a noble household. But taking place here in London in the midst of everyday life. Something that speaks to our common experiences and our everyday sorrows, joys and fears. And featuring characters with whom we are all familiar – young lovers, foolish old men, bawdy wenches and comic widows. In the end, they all get their just deserts and everything is set to rights!"

"Master Fletcher is an exponent of the New Comedy, Nat," said Master Beaumont with a smile. "It is quite different in style from these ponderous histories."

"Quite so!" he agreed. "It is based upon the plays of the Roman writer Plautus. He set his comedies in his contemporary society. His characters typically featured old men, young lovers and wily servants. We should write the same sorts of comedies for our own society. There is plenty of dramatic scope in contemporary London and the playgoers would love it!"

"I have an idea for just such a drama," said Master Beaumont. "It is a satirical comedy called *The Knight of the Burning Pestle*." I was hoping that you would assist me in writing it. We will share the risk and split the profits between us."

Master Fletcher was perfectly willing to collaborate in drafting a plot and writing a script. He had just written a play called "*The Faithful Shepherdess*," but it had proved a flop. "I fear that the title misled the playgoers into thinking it would be a pretty pastoral story about the lives of shepherds and their rustic sweethearts. I should have made better use of the Prologue to explain that it was a tragicomedy. Then it might have been a success!"

Consequently, he was looking for a new project. For the next week they spent every afternoon at the Mermaid thrashing out ideas. Then they divided the sections of the play between them. Master Beaumont preferred to do his writing at the tavern despite the interruptions. I often joined him there and contributed my own ideas for comic scenes. Thereafter, I developed a secret ambition of my own to write a play and have it performed on the stage.

When "*The Knight of the Burning Pestle*" was completed, it was offered to the Blackfriars company. I played the role of Rafe, the knight errant, and found the script very amusing. It began with the device of a play within a play and I thought it most diverting. Unfortunately, it was not a success with the playgoers. Master Kendall had to withdraw it from performance and substitute "*The Spanish Tragedy*" instead. The playwrights and I retired to the Mermaid to drown our sorrows.

Master Beaumont was deeply disappointed by the failure of his first play. "I don't understand," he sighed. "I thought that it was bound to captivate the audience."

"All the players liked it," I assured him. "But it was too sophisticated for the playgoers. They did not understand your clever humour."

"It's true," agreed Master Fletcher. "They have appalling taste and prefer a simple farce or ranting drama. They would rather see "*Titus Andronicus*" or "*Jeronimo*" than anything new and original!"

"Then I shall just have to adapt myself," he said. "After all, I'm not writing for the university wits at the colleges, but the good citizens of London. Most of them have never read a book or composed a verse."

"Don't be too disheartened, my friend," said Master Fletcher. "It happens to us all. The most important thing is that you have the talent to write. You will just have to try again. Playwrights are like tailors who work with an eye to the fashion."

Master Beaumont poured another draught of wine into his cup and banged down the flagon. "You are right! I shall have to think of something that will capture their fancy!"

The hearth crackled, casting shadows on the worn oak tables. I looked around the tavern wondering if Master Jonson would make an appearance. He would surely know the best way to encourage my friends. But he must have gone to visit the Mitre that night. There were no other writers present that evening to express their goodwill. It occurred to me that I had never seen Master Shakespeare there at all.

"I've never seen Master Shakespeare in the Mermaid. Where does he go?" I asked them.

"He's not one to spend his time sitting around in taverns. He's too busy with his writing."

I was disappointed to hear that I was not likely to have the chance to see Master Shakespeare again. I would have liked to hear his views on plays and the theatre. He was a master playwright whose comedies bore poignant undertones and whose tragedies echoed with laughter. But I did not want to offend my new friends. They regarded themselves as being the future of the theatre and their talents far surpassed my own. I knew that they could teach me the skills of how to write a witty comedy. Soon I would be ready to take up my quill and pen my own drama. My characters would be pretty daughters, foolish old fathers and devious young gallants. The schemes of the young would outwit the plans of the old, love would triumph over folly and the play would end with happy marriages. One day it would be my turn to present my own play at Blackfriars theatre and hear the laughter and applause from the crowd!

CHAPTER 7

The Dangers of Satire

"Those who have offended in lewd words, which is the children of Blackfriars, the king has vowed that they should never play more but should first beg their bread"

(Letter of King James I to the Privy Council, March 1608)

The court was the best route to patronage and fame for a playwright. Master Jonson and Samuel Daniel soon embarked upon a bitter rivalry to become the most favoured writer of the new king and queen. Master Daniel followed up his success with the queen's masque by writing a new play called *"The Tragedy of Philotas."* It told the story of an ambitious general who had plotted against the life of King Alexander the Great and was executed. The play was presented to the public at Blackfriars theatres where it proved to be extremely popular. Then it was performed at court on 3rd January 1605. But the play was not well received there. Many people at court felt that it drew too close a parallel with the rebellion of the earl of Essex in 1601. He was another ambitious general who had plotted to seize power from the rightful queen and had been executed for treason. Lord Thomas Howard, the Lord Chamberlain, reprimanded Master Daniel and Master Kendall for their temerity in showing such a play on the public stage and their folly in presenting it at court.

Master Daniel tried to plead his case. "My lord, this is an historical play set in ancient Greece. It is drawn from Plutarch's "*Life of Alexander the Great*." It makes no comparisons with any recent events in London."

"Do you take me for a buffoon, Master Daniel?" he snapped. "Every tavern in London has been set humming by your play! It has aroused recollections of the late rebellion which were better forgotten. Playgoers are drinking toasts to the memory of the earl of Essex and swearing that he was condemned as unjustly as General Philotas!"

"I am very sorry to hear such a report, my lord," he said, wringing his hands together. "Such an interpretation was never in my mind. I fear that the meaning of my play has been twisted by malcontents."

"Your protestations are idle, Master Daniel," he retorted. "Be warned that you will try my patience too far! Essex was no popular hero, but a rebel and a traitor! It is well-known that he wore the crown in his heart for many years before he tried to incite the citizens to march on Westminster!"

"Yes, of course, my lord," he replied. "I offer my most humble apologies."

"And I am surprised at you, Master Kendall. I would have thought that you had better judgement than to set your company of boys to present such a contentious subject!"

"I assure you, my lord, I had no notion that any unfortunate parallels could be drawn from the play."

"Indeed? Then, you must be a bigger fool than you look!" he barked. "As you well know, there is a law which forbids plays from dealing with matters of religion and the state! Playwrights cannot be permitted to stir up the playgoers and create civil discord! There have already been enough plots for the Privy Council to manage. I shall report this matter and you will be summoned to appear before them. In the meantime, I caution you to stay away from politics in future and write your plays for entertainment!"

As soon as the Lord Chancellor left, Master Daniel collapsed into a chair. His face had turned ashen. Master Kendall hastened to bring him a goblet of wine. Master Daniel clutched at his arm in distress.

"This is a disaster! Whatever shall I say to the Privy Council?" he lamented.

"Try to touch their hearts, Master Daniel. Tell them that you wrote the play out of dire necessity."

"Yes, yes!" he agreed. "I shall ask them to take pity on me. I will promise to withdraw my play and keep to my house until the scandal has been forgotten. Surely that will content them!"

And so, it proved to be. Master Kendall was relieved that the matter was dropped. He began rehearsals for a new play at once. This time it was a harmless comedy called "*All Fools*."

At first, Master Jonson was amused to hear of the sorry predicament of his rival. He drank a toast at the Mermaid tavern to wish him a long and pleasant retirement from the stage. But then he turned sober and said that it was no jest after all, but a matter to concern all playwrights. "Take heed, the days are grown dangerous," he muttered.

"What do you mean?" I asked him. It was no new thing for plays to stir up controversies. Master Daniel had denied that any allegory was intended. But I did not think that he was as innocent as he claimed to be.

"Are we then to have no discourse upon serious matters?" he declared. "Are we not free to dramatize episodes from the chronicles if we cannot treat of the history of our own times? Are we to make children of our citizens? The Privy Councillors would have the people's eyes turned away from their injustices and abuses and beguiled with pleasant fancies. But that is not our part. We cannot always be writing about weddings, pageants and celebrations. The court censors would place a yoke upon our necks. But we may still contrive to evade them!"

He took a draught of his favourite canary wine. It was evident that he felt strongly about the subject of censorship and was in the humour to discourse at length. He sighed and his mood turned pensive.

"In my youth, I once took it into my head to compose a play on the life of Sir Thomas More. I don't know what folly possessed me! When I showed it to Sir Edmund Tilney, he sucked his teeth and then cut it all to pieces. I could not portray his quelling of the riots on Evil May Day for it was too dangerous to show rioting on the streets of London. Nor could I mention that he had been executed for refusing the sign the Oath of Supremacy. As if all of London had not seen his head rotting on London Bridge! He advised me to begin with his work at the mayor's sessions and show his rise in the king's favour as a Privy Counsellor and Lord Chancellor. Then I should finish the play with a commendation of his good service. I was not to do otherwise at my own peril. So, I had to give it up as a bad job. There are some subjects that cannot be handled, even today!"

But despite Master Jonson's sense of pique, his fortunes turned sooner than he had expected. The queen had not forgotten the outdoor masque which had been performed for her entertainment at Althorpe. She sent for him and gave him a commission for a masque to be performed during the Christmas celebrations. Master Jonson was in the best of humours again. He was soon hard at work writing the speeches.

"The queen wishes me to write her next masque," he told me proudly. "It will be performed before the court at the banqueting hall at Whitehall Palace on Twelfth Night."

"What do you intend for your masque?" I asked Master Jonson. I wondered how he intended to outdo Master Daniel in his production.

"Its purpose is to glorify and affirm the monarch," he replied. "The Master of the Revels will organise the music, the dancers and the costumes for the performance. Master Inigo Jones will design the scenery for the stage. But it is my task to write the verse. That is the very spirit of the masque. The rest is but the carcass."

"So, what is the story?" I enquired. I wondered if he intended to take a classical theme or recount a popular legend.

It will be called "*A Masque of Blacknesse*," he replied. "The queen will appear as Euphoria and her ladies as the daughters of the River Niger. The masque will begin with the River Niger talking to his father Oceanus. He will tell him that his daughters are troubled because they had thought themselves to be the most beautiful goddesses in the world, but now they feared that this was no longer true. Then the moon goddess, Aethiopia, will appear in her white and silver garb. She will advise him that if his daughters can find a country named Britannia and dance before its king, they would be beautiful once more."

"I hope you have got a part in it for me," I said. I did not want to miss such an opportunity.

"Of course, Nat," he replied. "You shall play the role of the moon goddess, Aethiopia." I could not have been happier. In addition to the pleasure of visiting Whitehall palace and performing before the king and his court, I would be paid a fee of four pounds.

Queen Anne wished this masque to be even more memorable than the first one had been. And, indeed it was. The scenery of the masque was quite spectacular. The image of a stormy sea was created using flowing blue cloths that moved like waves. The queen and her ladies arrived in a great scalloped seashell drawn by seahorses which seemed to float upon the water. They were dressed in flimsy gowns of silver and azure with pearls and feathers in their hair. They were accompanied by six large sea monsters carrying torchbearers dressed in green doublets with gold sleeves. The ladies travelled to Mauritania, Lusitania and Aquitania. Finally, they reached Britannia, the land that was ruled by the sun. The queen and her ladies stepped out of their seashell and processed onto the stage in pairs. Each lady displayed a fan with her name on it. They celebrated their arrival with an interweaving circle dance. Then they partnered with blue-skinned mermen and performed several measures and corantoes. At the end of the masque, I stepped forward and made my speech in praise of the king:

> *"The sacred Muses' sons have honoured,*
> *And from bright Hesperus to Eous spread.*
> *With that great name Britannia, this blest isle*
> *Hath won her ancient dignity, and style,*
> *A world divided from the world: and tried*
> *The abstract of it, in his general pride.*
> *For were the world, with all his wealth, a ring,*
> *Britannia, whose new name makes all tongues sing,*
> *Might be a diamant worthy to inchase it,*
> *Ruled by a sun, that to this height doth grace it."*

King James watched the performance from a raised dais. Next to him sat the ambassadors of Spain and Venice. I could tell that he was flattered by being described as a sun king. He sat up straighter on his chair of estate and raised his head as though he could indeed radiate beams of light upon his supplicants. The masque was followed by a general revel which lasted for several hours. I amused myself by watching the great lords and ladies of the court as they tripped about the hall. The queen danced with the Spanish ambassador who rose to the occasion nobly. Finally, the trumpets blew to signal that the banquet was ready. Unfortunately, the announcement prompted a rush of people to reach the tables. They had been spread with a splendid array of jellies of all colours, fruit tarts and suckets, gilded marchpane and sugared cotignac. However, such was the press of the crowd that the trestles collapsed sending the fine dishes crashing to the floor. The queen was vexed by the dismal end to her splendid masque.

CHAPTER 8

Interlude in a Prison

"Stone Walls doe not a Prison make,
Nor Iron bars a Cage;
Mindes innocent and quiet take
That for an Hermitage;
If I have freedome in my Love,
And in my soule am free;
Angels alone that sore above,
Injoy such Liberty."

("To Althea, From Prison," Richard Lovelace, 1642).

In August 1605, the royal family decided to go on a visit to Oxford and make a tour of the university colleges. The university canons wanted to honour them with a special entertainment at Christ College. So, they commissioned Samuel Daniel to write a new play for the occasion. He presented a simple pastoral drama called *"The Queen's Arcadia."* It described how a pair of villains tried to corrupt the harmony of Arcadia, but were defeated in their wicked designs. The occasion was applauded as a great success. But Master Jonson was annoyed to have been passed over. "It is a few Italian herbs picked up and made into a salad!" he said dismissively.

He followed up his court masque by presenting a new play at Blackfriars theatre called "*Eastwood Ho!*" It was a city comedy about a London goldsmith called Touchstone. He encouraged his daughter Gertrude to marry Sir Petronel Flash in the belief that he was a wealthy nobleman. However, it turned out that he was neither rich nor noble, but only a "thirty-pound knight." I played the comic role of the First Gentleman with a broad Scottish accent who mocked the pretentious knight. There had been complaints at court about the king's Scottish favourites and the selling of knighthoods and the audience laughed heartily at the jest. But one man was not laughing. He was a courtier named Sir James Murray who had been knighted by King James. He admonished Master Kendall for his audacity in putting such a play on the public stage.

"How dare you speak of thirty-pound knights!" he declared. "It is a stain upon the king's honour! His Majesty shall hear of this insult and he will be greatly moved to anger!"

Master Kendall was furious with Master Jonson. "Which one of your friends at court bribed you to include that foolish jibe against the Scots?" he demanded. "It will cost us dear."

Master Jonson was remarkably sanguine in the face of this disaster. "At the coronation of King James, it was common knowledge that he knighted any man who bribed his friends for the privilege. He took no account of whether they were worthy gentlemen or sheep-reeves, yeomen's sons or pedlar's sons. He did not even draw the line at honouring Thimblethorpe the attorney - a man who is better known as Nimblechops full of the pox! He got his knighthood for the price of seven pounds and ten shillings. Should we disregard the corruption of the court or seek to remedy it?"

"Let others remedy it, Master Jonson," he railed at him. "We are but simple men. Now we shall forfeit the favour of the king and queen!"

"Comic satires are what the playgoers of London come here to see, Master Kendall! Would you rather I wrote some feeble nonsense like Philip Sidney's "*Arcadia*"?" he demanded. "All the gallants of London would laugh at us and take their custom elsewhere!"

"Well, they won't see anything if we are closed down," he grumbled.

But worse was in store. The Lord Chamberlain was ordered to make an example of the playwright and the players who were responsible for embarrassing his Majesty. The following day Master Jonson and I were arrested for lewd and mutinous behaviour.

"Why are you taking me?" I protested. "What have I done?"

"Did you not play the role of the First Gentleman in "*Eastwood Ho!*"?"

"Yes, I did," I admitted.

"You have seditiously traduced his Majesty in public," he replied. "You deserve to stand in the pillory and have both your ears lopped off!"

We were taken to the Marshalsea prison in Southwark. It was a crumbling brick building with a notorious reputation. On our arrival the gaoler unlocked the padlock to the common cell and swung open the door. We recoiled from the stench that filled our nostrils as we stepped inside. The reeds which covered the floor were old and rancid. He grinned to see our appalled expressions as we took in our surroundings. I had never seen such squalor. It seemed that the most miserable specimens of humanity had been gathered from the alleys of London and crammed inside. Some wore fetters on their ankles. Most were dressed in rags. They stared back at us apathetically. But a few of the sunken eyes took on an avid look as they appraised our fine garments. Master Jonson sensed our danger and placed his boot in the door.

"A word with you, my good man," he said ingratiatingly. "I am sure that you have more suitable lodgings available."

"Well, that's according," he replied, with a knowing smirk.

"I am no common felon, but a man of substance," he continued." I have powerful friends who stand ready to assist me."

The goaler did not move an inch. Master Jonson sighed and drew the gold pin from his doublet. "Will this suffice?" he asked.

The goaler closed his hand around it and heaved the door open. "Follow me," he said. He led us out into the open courtyard. It was a blessed relief to be out in the fresh air and light again. He took us over to the Master's side of the prison and placed us in a cell that had pallets with blankets, wooden stools and a candle. At that moment, it seemed like a vision of paradise.

"This is where the offenders of quality lodge," he assured him. "But you have to pay rent to live in here. Two shillings a week."

"You may rely upon me, my good fellow," Master Jonson replied. He heaved a sigh and seated himself precariously upon the larger of the two stools. I took the other one. At least we now had a clean floor and a bed. I was so weary that I could have slept upon a plank.

He sighed. "It was an extravagance," he said. "But needs must when the devil drives. A night in that place would have done for us both."

"We would either have come down with prison fever or had our heads broken for the sake of our boots," I agreed. I was grateful that Master Jonson was a man of enterprise when he found himself in a tight corner.

"I am sorry it has come to this, Nat," he said. "I would not for the world have brought you to such a miserable place. But this is only a temporary setback. As soon as my friends know of my plight, they will petition the Lord Chamberlain to have us released." He knocked on the door and asked the gaoler to provide him with parchment, quills and ink.

"Mostly, I get asked for meat pasties and canary wine," he replied in surprise. "My boy here can supply all your wants as long as you have the coin for it."

"My good man, I was brought here in such a hurried manner that I have no coin upon me. I need the parchment in order to write to my friends for assistance. I can assure you that I will faithfully repay everything that I owe you."

"No coin, no favours," snapped the gaoler and walked away.

Master Jonson was furious. "I thought he was a reasonable man, but he is as great a rogue as any of the king's courtiers. We shall have to wait until my friends seek me out, Nat."

But our first visitor turned out to be my brother Theophilus. He bribed the goaler to bring me out into the prison courtyard. He looked around in disgust at my sorry circumstances.

"Well Nat, I am sorry indeed to see you here," he sighed. I looked at his face. His expression showed that it was only what he had expected.

"I have come at our mother's bidding," he informed me. "I can only hope this experience has opened your eyes, Nat. It is high time that you changed your way of life. When you get out of here you should leave your company of players and go to live with our mother. Then you can take up an honest profession. Our brother Nathaniel is now a stationer and doing very well. There is no reason that you could not do the same."

But that was not for me. I had tasted the sweets of performing for the playgoers of London and the royal court. How could I give all that up for the tedium of being a clerk? How could I leave all my friends? I wanted to learn how to be a writer and see my own plays performed on the stage. No, I could not give that up. Better to brave the hazards and hope for better days to come.

"It is just a misunderstanding," I insisted. "Master Jonson's friends will soon rectify it."

"It seems to me that Master Jonson is the one who has led you astray. But if you want to play the part of the prodigal son, on your head be it!" He concluded his visit by giving me five shillings to purchase necessities.

"Don't spend it all on drink, Nat," he admonished me. I spent it on a stock of parchment and quills so that Master Jonson could petition his friends. The goalers boy was duly despatched on his errand and Master Jonson cheered up at the sight of them. A further shilling persuaded the gaoler to loan him the use of a table.

"Here, Nat, you take this down while I frame my thoughts," he said. "I shall send my appeal to Lord Robert Cecil, the earl of Salisbury, for he is the most powerful man in the kingdom."

"To the most noble, virtuous and thrice-honoured earl of Salisbury," he began. "Most honoured lord, I am committed to a vile prison and with me, Master Nathan Field, a learned and honest man. The cause of our imprisonment is a play, my lord. I pray that your lordship will be the most honoured cause of our liberty. Whereby you shall bind us and our muses to the thankful honouring of you and yours to posterity; as your own virtues have by many descents of ancestors ennobled you to time. Your Honour's most devoted servant in heart and words, Ben Jonson."

"There! I hope that it shall serve our turn," he muttered. "But just in case it does not, I shall despatch some others to accompany it."

Master Jonson dictated a series of further missives and gave them to the boy to deliver to his friends. He told him to call at the Mitre tavern and bring us a couple of hot pasties and bottles of beer on his way back. He had regained his usual confidence.

"These are the buffets of life and we must stand against them boldly. You cannot learn this lesson too young!" he declared. "Besides, this is all grist to the mill for a dramatist. In time I shall make good use of this experience." That night we spent a merry night in our squalid cell. I looked forward to being released in a few days' time. But his friends were less effective that Master Jonson had hoped. The weeks turned into months and we were still incarcerated. Master Jonson was downcast at the lack of result. But he was not the kind of man to admit defeat.

"We must not waste the time that we have. We must make best use of it. And the best use of time is education and study. I shall teach you how to frame a play."

My heart leaped within me. It was my dearest desire to write a play of my own. But it would not be an ancient tragedy or an historical drama. It would be a comedy in which the characters' lives would intertwine, unravel and then triumphantly conclude with a happy ending. I would keep the audience entertained with witty dialogues and farcical situations. It was a thrilling prospect.

"A good play should be like a good woollen cloth, well woven without any breaks, holes or loose ends in it, or like a good picture which has been well-painted and designed," he began, his great brow creasing as he considered his theme. "The playwright must conceive of the plot or contrivement, the design, the writing, the colours, and counterplot, the shadowings, and other embellishments. It may be compared to well contrived garden which is cast into walks and counter-walks, between an alley and a wilderness, neither too plain, nor too confused. The audience should be led in a maze, but not a mist; and through turning and winding ways until they find their way at last to the destination. A play can ask questions that are hard to answer. It can reveal the truth about being human. It can illuminate the secrets of the human heart and reveal the hidden jealousies and hatreds that burn within.

He paused briefly, as I listened to him enthralled. At that moment, I would not have exchanged places with the richest man in London. "Of all the arts, that of the dramatic poet is the most difficult and the most subject to censure; for the poet must write of everything, and every one undertakes to judge of it. A dramatic poet is to the stage as a pilot to the ship; and to the actors, as a master to his scholars. He is to be a good moral philosopher, but more learned in men than books. He is to be a wise, as well as a witty man, and a good man, as well as a good poet; and I'd allow him to be so far a good fellow as to take a cheerful cup to whet his wits. So, pour us both another glass of beer, Nat. Then we will continue further."

I hastened to bring him a drink as I did not want to break the thread of his discourse. The days no longer seemed long to me as I sat as Master Jonson's feet and listened to his golden words. He discoursed to me at length about the works of Plautus and Terence, his favourite Roman playwrights. Then he discussed the Elizabethan playwrights of greatest renown before proceeding onto the works of his contemporaries. Finally, he took his own plays one by one and outlined their theme and their plot, enumerating their dramatic and comic devices. He explained to me how to build up a story to a dramatic denouement and to make use of a variety of scenarios in order to captivate the audience. A skilled playwright employed dramatic duels and tavern brawls, false marriages and disguisings to heighten the tension. A play should also offer spectacle so there should be space for music, songs and dancing. Above all, he believed that a play should be a mirror of men's lives and actions. He did not write his plays merely to entertain the crowds. He wished his plays to resonate with a higher meaning. So, he did not limit himself to penning great historical tragedies. A number of his plays were comedies set among the taverns, shops and streets of London. I was inspired to hear of his great work as a dramatist.

"My ambition is to live to perfect such a work myself," I declared. I had performed in numerous plays as an actor. So I had a good understanding of what pleased an audience.

"You should use this time to plan your own dramatic work, Nat. I have given you the tools. Now it is up to you. What would you choose to write about?"

"I would set it in London among the common people. It would be a comedy of manners," I replied.

"But what would be your theme?" he demanded. "What is the point of your play? Is it merely to entertain the crowd? No, it must have a higher purpose. You must seek to remedy society's ills under the guise of humour!"

I was dumbfounded. It seemed that there were underlying messages even in a comic play. I contemplated what should be my central theme. Love? Betrayal? Redemption? The possibilities were endless.

"If I had my books here with me, I would show you. But you have performed in *"Cynthia's Revels.*" What did you think was the deeper theme?"

"To honour her Majesty the Queen?" I replied.

"Yes, without a doubt. But it was also an oblique satire on the court. The foolish courtiers were not only there for comedy. They were intended to ridicule those who sought undeserved favour at the court. A play can act as a mirror upon society. A playwright knows how to reflect its errors as well as celebrate its glories. Our plays express the truth under the cover of entertainment. And our words have the power to shake the thrones of monarchs. But such a calling has its risks. It is like walking along a tightrope. You may gain or lose favour at a stroke."

"As you did with "*Eastwood Ho!*"" I could not help pointing out.

He sighed. "Yes, indeed, I was too bold and forthright. It touched the king too near. His patronage of the Scots was too sensitive a matter for comic banter. I should have been more delicate in my allusions. Indeed, satire is the most subtle of all the arts."

In October, Master Jonson's friends at court managed to intercede with the king. We were released from prison and returned back to Blackfriars. It seemed that everything had been put to rights. Master Jonson held a banquet to celebrate and invited all his friends to come. But the following month another drama occurred. This time it was serious enough to shake the whole nation.

CHAPTER 9

The Gunpowder Plot (5th November 1505)

*"Remember, remember, the fifth of November, the gunpowder treason and plot.
I see no reason why gunpowder treason should ever be forgot!"*

(Traditional English rhyme)

On 5th November 1605 a man named Guy Fawkes was discovered hiding in the under croft of Westminster Hall with thirty-six barrels of gunpowder. He was arrested for plotting to blow up Parliament and kill King James and his government. The news caused a great sensation in London and all the church bells were rung in thanksgiving for his deliverance. The following Sunday, everyone attended church to show their loyalty and hear what the minister had to say about the plot. Jack and I dressed in our best clothes and hurried around to St Saviour's church in good time. But the pews were already crammed with bodies. We were forced to stand at the back. The minister looked gratified to see such a great congregation. "Today I shall take as my theme the book of Esther chapter seven." *Haman*, I thought. I was not disappointed.

"Then Harbonah, one of the eunuchs attending the king, said: There is a **gallows** fifty cubits high at Haman's house. He had it built for Mordecai, who gave the report that saved the king." "Hang him on it!" declared the king. So, they hanged Haman on the gallows he had prepared for Mordecai. Then the fury of the king subsided." The congregation nodded their approval.

"We must be grateful today that our king and our Parliament have experienced a similar great deliverance from evil. If the traitors had succeeded in their vile plot, then the greatest men in the kingdom and all the bishops of the church would now lie slain." The congregation listened with solemn faces. Jack dug me in the ribs. "He might have got his preferment," he whispered. I controlled my mirth and kept a straight face for the church warden was standing nearby clutching his wand of office.

"The plan was to have blown up the king at the time he was set on his royal throne accompanied by his sons, the nobility and commoners and attended by the bishops, judges and doctors. At one stroke it would have ruined the whole state and kingdom of England. But fortunately, the plotters were discovered in time and their wicked designs were prevented. The king has decreed that henceforth the fifth of November shall be celebrated as a day of special prayer and thanksgiving by his loyal subjects." The congregation applauded. I reflected that if my father had lived, I would undoubtedly have entered the church like my older brother Theophilus. I was certain that I could preach as good a sermon as our minister. Fortunately, my family had such staunch Puritan credentials that none of us were in danger of arrest. But many other suspects were being rounded up. Two months later, Jack Underwood sought me out.

"The conspirators are going to be put on trial at Westminster Hall, Nat. We should attend the hearings. They're bound to cause a great sensation!"

Chapter 9: The Gunpowder Plot (5th November 1505) | 123

The streets of Westminster were crowded with people waiting to jeer the conspirators as they were brought from the Tower to stand trial. Ballad-mongers were already hawking their verses and bawling them out at the top of their voices:

"Remember, remember,
The fifth of November,
The gunpowder treason and plot;
I'll tell you a reason,
Why gunpowder treason,
Should never be forgot.

If there hadn't been given,
Protection from Heaven,
To the Parliament Houses and throne
When the Pope to the flames,
Had devoted King James,
They had all to destruction been blown.

Then ever let England her gratitude shew,
To the Power that saved her that horrible blow;
Our voices with thankfulness loud let us raise,
To Him be the glory—to Him be the praise."

Westminster Hall was draped with hangings of black velvet so that it resembled the stage of a tragedy play. An immense throng of people filled the hall. Jack and I crammed ourselves into the heaving mass and wriggled our way forward until we could get a view of the proceedings. The conspirators were brought into the hall and displayed to the crowds on a purpose-built scaffold. At the sight of them the crowds shouted, "Villains! Murderers! Send them to Tyburn!" Some of the men looked to be in a very poor condition.

"Do you think they've been tortured?" I asked Jack.

"Of course they have," he replied with satisfaction. "They've been stretched on the rack to make them confess."

The conspirators were a group of English Catholics who wanted greater religious tolerance. In the Tower they confessed that they had intended to kill King James and Prince Henry. They meant to capture the young Princess Elizabeth and set her up as the new head of state. Guy Fawkes pleaded not guilty to the charges, despite being caught red-handed at the scene with a match and a watch. But he and the rest of the conspirators were found guilty of high treason and sentenced to be hanged, drawn and quartered.

"It would certainly make a marvellous play!" I reflected as we walked back to Blackfriars.

"Are you mad?" he replied scornfully. "The authorities would never allow it to be performed. It would be labour in vain!"

"Then it could be used as the basis for a conspiracy in Ancient Greece or Rome. Everyone would see the parallels and the groundlings would love it."

"Only if you waited for a few years for the scandal to die down. Otherwise, it could be seen as sedition against the king and his government."

"An adept writer can always get around the censors and at the same time hold a mirror up to society. As long as the play is set in the distant past and it ends with a good moral, the censors won't recognise the satire. In fact, they will take it as a loyal tribute to the government." But I was over-optimistic and Jack had a better understanding of the times in which we lived. I took his point when we performed our next play at Blackfriars.

In March 1606 I was cast as the lead in a new play called *"The Isle of Gulls."* The playwright, John Day, was eager to make a name for himself as a daring and provocative author. The play was a satirical comedy which lampooned King James for neglecting the affairs of state for the pleasures of hunting. His court favourites were ridiculed as "worms who eat into the credit of the nobility." And it expressed the desire to expel the Scots from England. The audience roared their approval and the play was a great success. However, King James was fervently committed to unite England and Scotland into one nation under his rule. He had already told Parliament, "I am the husband and the whole isle is my lawful wife." When news of the controversial play reached court, the king was furious. Lord Thomas Howard, the Lord Chamberlain, came to Blackfriars in person to censure Master Kendall for his insolence.

"Why did you not show this play to me before putting it before the public? You have disobeyed the regulations!" he declared in agitation.

"It was an unfortunate oversight, my lord. You were out of the city at the time."

"This is a fine state of affairs, Master Kendall. The king is furious with you. He considers it to be a seditious prelude to put into people's heads boldness and faction."

"I regret that our new play should have displeased him so greatly."

"What did you expect? I looked for better judgement from a man of your experience. Now you will have to pay the price for your folly!"

"What do you mean, your lordship?"

"I mean that this play is closed and your theatre is closed!"

"But what about the players?"

"The king has said that he does not care if the players are forced to beg their bread upon the streets. Good day!" He swept out of the office leaving Master Kendall pale and quaking.

"We are ruined! That fool of a playwright has destroyed us all!"

"At least he did not have us arrested for treason."

"A cold comfort, Nat," he replied.

"What shall we do?" I asked him. It seemed like the death-knell of our company had sounded. I wondered what would become of us.

"I will contrive something. Perhaps a short tour of the provinces would be timely. It will allow time for the king's anger to cool. On our return, we can petition for his gracious mercy." He mopped his brow with his handkerchief. But Master Kendall was a most resourceful man. He had learned how to bend with the winds of fortune. On our return to London from our tour, he ingeniously renamed the company as "*The Children of the Revels.*" Soon we re-opened our theatre and were as popular as ever.

Master Jonson soon returned to royal favour after his time in prison and he was given a new commission. King Christian of Denmark was making a state visit to England in the summer of 1606. King James had invited him to join their annual progress during which he would be entertained at Theobalds House. Queen Anna intended to impress him with a splendid performance of "*Solomon and Sheba.*" Master Jonson was pleased to be offered a theme which offered him the scope for designing grand spectacles and writing notable speeches. He was confident of a great success. By now he regarded me as his protégé. So, he invited me to accompany him to Theobalds as his assistant. I was only too pleased to accept his offer.

"Are you bringing some of the others in the company to recite the verses?" I enquired.

"Not on this occasion, Nat," he replied. "There will be no need of any actors because the queen and her ladies wish to give the speeches themselves."

"You mean the ladies intend to perform upon the stage!" I exclaimed. "Surely, the king will not approve!"

"Well, this is a private entertainment, so the king will wink his eye at it," he explained.

We accompanied the two kings and their courtiers on their journey from London to Theobalds House. The owner, Lord Salisbury, had spared no expense for the occasion. The road to the entrance was strewn with artificial green leaves. At the gates stood an artificial tree with green silk leaves and a banner reading *Welcome* in gold letters. At the porch of the house were three Hours sitting upon clouds. Their names were Law, Justice and Peace. They stood and made a speech of welcome to their royal guests. Theobalds was renowned as the most splendid residence in England. It was said that the king had designs upon it because he considered it too magnificent for a mere subject. And its parklands had some of the best hunting in the kingdom. I had thought that Hardwick Hall was the most impressive house in England. But Theobalds far exceeded it in splendour. The Presence Chamber was decorated with oak trees. The ceiling was painted with the sun, the stars and the signs of the zodiac. The cream of the court was gathered there to greet the two kings. I gaped to see the multitude of jewels on display and the glorious spangles and rich embroidery of the clothes. The queen wore a white satin gown embroidered with pearls and coloured silks.

Master Jonson shot me a quizzical look. "Tis but borrowed finery. The whole court is ablaze with jewels not yet paid for! Do you know why courtiers are like peddlers? It is because they carry their whole estates upon their backs!"

I was somewhat disillusioned, but still entranced by the splendid dancing which followed. The courtiers danced the stately pavane, the lively galliard and the daring volta. A great entertainment had been prepared for the two kings with good meat, good drink, and good speeches. On the final day a great banquet was held for the company. Afterwards, the representation of *"Solomon and Sheba"* was presented before their Majesties. But I had never seen a performance go more awry! The lady who played the part of Queen Sheba was supposed to bring precious gifts to their Majesties. However, she tripped on the steps to the canopy, tipped her caskets into King Christian's lap and fell at his feet. Then King James got up saying that he would dance with the Queen of Sheba; but fell down in front of her. He was carried away and laid upon a bed of state.

I thought that the masque would be abandoned, but the queen signalled for it to continue. The entertainment went forward, but most of the presenters were completely overcome with wine. They could hardly keep on their feet, let alone speak their lines. First, three ladies in rich dress appeared as Hope, Faith, and Charity. Hope attempted to speak, but wine rendered her so incoherent that she was forced to withdraw. Faith came to the king's feet, made obeisance and brought gifts. But she said she would return home again, as there was no gift which heaven had not already given his Majesty. Charity was left all alone and departed the court in a staggering condition. She joined Hope and Faith, who were both sick and spewing in the lower hall. Next came Victory, in bright armour who presented a rich sword to the king. But after much lamentable utterance she was led away and laid to sleep in the outer steps of the anti-chamber. Finally, Peace entered, but quarrelled with her attendants; and laid her olive branch on their pates.

I thought that it was the funniest thing I had seen in a twelvemonth and better than any farce at the Globe. I would not have missed it for worlds. But Master Jonson looked mortified. He had been expecting to receive the gracious praise of the monarchs. Instead, King Christian was so disguised that he tried to make love to the Countess of Nottingham, causing a quarrel with her husband. The masque ended in a shambles as Lady Arbella tried to make peace between the two men. On our journey back to London the following day, Master Jonson was sunk in a gloomy silence. He felt that he had wasted his labours.

"Are you quite well, Master Jonson," I ventured.

He sighed and mopped his brow. "Whenever I presented an entertainment at the royal palaces they were always conducted with taste and decorum. But now they have degenerated into bawdy revels. Never did I see such a lack of good order, discretion, and sobriety. There was hardly a man or a woman present who could command themselves. I wished that I was back at home. It is my one consolation that it did not take place at Hampton Court or else it would be the common talk of London."

"It seems that they enjoyed the banquet too much to manage their performances," I replied. "But this is what happens when amateurs take it upon themselves to perform upon the stage. You should have arranged for our company to perform the masque. It would have spared you from embarrassment."

"That is how it would have been done in the days of Good Queen Bess. But now the ladies of the court want their chance to dress up and show themselves off. And since it was a private house, their wishes could not well be denied. But the remembrance of it makes me shudder even now! I only hope there will be no repetition. I cannot imagine what King Christian must have thought of us!"

"Perhaps it is quite the custom at the Danish court?" I suggested.

He snorted. "I cannot believe any monarch who respected himself would encourage such carouses. His attendants must be laughing up their sleeves at us. When he returns to Denmark, we shall be the laughing stock of Europe! The worst of it is that King James seems quite oblivious to the impression he has made. I am going away tomorrow to take the hot waters at Bath so I can forget what has passed and recover my spirits. By the time I return I hope that his Majesty will have realised the folly of allowing the queen's ladies to speak in the masques and forbid it altogether!"

In 1607 King James decided that the old banqueting hall built by Queen Elizabeth was not worthy of displaying the splendid court masques. He ordered a new banqueting hall to be constructed out of stone. The following year it was completed and Queen Anna commissioned a new masque called *"The Masque of Beauty"* from Master Jonson. The queen and her ladies appeared as the daughters of the River Niger. They dressed in ornate gowns of orange, green and silver and sat upon a great throne upon a floating island. Among these favoured ladies was Lady Arbella. She had grown into a most beautiful young lady. She wore the most splendid jewels which were only surpassed by those of the queen.

The idea of the masque was very simple. Night yielded to day and darkness to beauty. The forces of earth, wind, fire and water were kept in harmony by the power of beauty and love. I played the role of Volturnus the Wind and made my speech to Master Thomas Giles who personified the River Thames. He held an urn which flowed with water and wore a robe of blue cloth of silver and a crown of flowers:

"Rise aged Thames, and by the hand
Receive these Nymphes, within the land:

And, in those curious Squares, and Rounds,
Wherewith thou flow'st betwixt the grounds,
Of fruitful Kent, and Essex faire,
That lend thee garlands for thy haire;
Instruct their silver feete to tread,
Whilst we, againe to sea, are fled."

My speech signalled the end of the spoken masque and the beginning of the dances. The queen and her ladies performed four elegant dances on the stage which so enchanted the king that he insisted that they were performed again. The ladies partnered with courtiers to perform a series of galliards and corantoes. Then the ladies retired to sit upon their throne of beauty. The formal dances were followed by a court revel and a banquet. This time the evening was a great success.

Now that I was older and played the role of handsome young gallants, the maids of honour no longer hovered around to pet me. Instead, they gave me sidelong looks of admiration and longing. I had been splendidly attired by the Master of the Revels for the role of Volturnus. My costume was as fine as that of any aspiring young courtier. I only wished that I could keep it. I suppose that I looked the very picture of a noble prince from the Song of Roland or a daring young knight from the tales of Camelot. I raised my head and gave a pensive smile and watched how they leaned in closer. I could see that they were imagining that they were Eleanor of Castile being serenaded by her troubadours in the days of chivalry. It was a shame that I was not the son of a nobleman for I was certain that I could pay my court to a lady better than any of the sullen-faced popinjays who hung about the king. If any of them tried to perform on the stage I was sure that they would make a sorry spectacle of themselves and be hissed by everyone. Master Jonson came hurrying over to me.

"Take care, Nat, or you'll provoke a quarrel!" he said good-humouredly. "These noble bloods are touchy about their ladies. You'll find it doesn't do to stir up envy at the court. Come with me and make your bow to the queen."

Queen Anna was so adorned for the occasion that she fairly glittered with jewels. Around her neck was a necklace that had belonged to Queen Mary Tudor. She was in raptures over the success of her masque. "Master Jonson, you have outdone yourself," she declared. "I have been showered with compliments from everyone. They say that everything was so delightful that they were quite transported by it. What a shame that it has to come to an end so soon!"

Master Jonson bowed at her compliments. "A masque is an ephemeral joy, your Majesty," he replied. "But it makes us look forward with greater anticipation to the pleasure of the next one."

"Yes indeed, Master Jonson," she agreed. "Lady Bedford and I must put our heads together and plan another idea for a masque. You can be sure of hearing from us in due course."

"I thank your Majesty," he answered and we withdrew.

"It could not have gone better, Nat!" he beamed. "Now I think we deserve a hearty cup of wine after our labours."

"Should we not attend on his Majesty too?" I asked.

"No, for it is the queen's own enterprise. To tell you the truth, the king is not much interested in masques or plays. He only really enjoys watching the dancing."

CHAPTER 10

The Playwright

"I have been vexed with vile plays myselfe, a great while, hearing many; nowe I thought to be even with some, and they should heare mine too"

(Preface to "A Woman is a Weathercocke", Nathan Field, 1612)

In 1608 a wealthy goldsmith named Master Robert Keysar bought up the shares in our company and became our new manager. Jack Underwood and William Ostler both left and joined the King's Men. But I stayed to become the leading player of this new company which took the name, *"The Children of Blackfriars."* In March 1608 we performed two new plays. The first was called "The Silver Mine." It portrayed King James as a pleasure-seeking drunkard. And it depicted his attempt to make money out of silver mines as a folly. A few days later, we staged *"Charles, Duke of Byron."* The subject was a French nobleman who rebelled against his lawful monarch. It included a scene in which the French queen slapped the face of the king's mistress. The French ambassador complained that this was outrageous. The king decided that enough was enough. As a sign of his displeasure, he ordered all the theatres in London to be closed. However, he relented in time for the court entertainments at Christmas to be presented. We performed three times at court during the Christmas celebrations of 1608.

I noticed a young man with fair hair and a pale complexion in close attendance on the king. He was dressed in very flamboyant clothes with splendid jewelled ornaments. The king frequently glanced in his direction and smiled at him. I wondered if he was a foreign prince to be shown such favour. Jack Underwood soon enlightened me. He prided himself on always knowing the latest gossip at court.

"That's the king's new favourite, Robert Carr," he said knowingly. "He is the younger son of a Scottish gentlemen and a complete nobody. He came to the king's attention in the most absurd manner. He fell off his horse at a joust and the king insisted on doctoring his wounds. They have been inseparable ever since. The king has taught him Latin and made him a knight. The rest of the court are furious about it because he has neither birth nor talent to recommend him."

I looked at him again, but he appeared the most ordinary of men. I would not have looked twice at him if it were not for his elaborate costume. At his belt he wore a tablet of gold with the king's image which was a mark of high favour. To my mind he lacked the self-assurance to make a successful player. Yet his face had made his fortune. It seemed like something out of a fairy tale.

Queen Anna wanted to present a sequel to the "*Masque of Beauty*." So, she commissioned Master Jonson to write the "*Masque of Queens*" in 1609. She would appear in it as Bel-Anna, the Queen of the Ocean. Above all, the masque was a showcase for her Majesty. I loved to watch the queen and her ladies practicing their dancing. Their patience was remarkable as they rehearsed their steps time and again. They were determined to impress the king and the court with their grace and dexterity. The challenge for Master Jonson was to make each masque seem even more elaborate than the one before.

"I have a new conceit," said Master Jonson in triumph. "It is an anti-masque. A group of masquers will perform a dance which serves as a contrast to the queen's dance. This introductory dance will feature a dance of witches in hell!"

"Why do you want to include witches?" I asked him.

"The king is very interested in witchcraft," he replied. "He considers himself an expert on the subject. We must consider his tastes as well as those of the queen. I shall tell the Master of the Revels that he must commission strange music and have the dancers perform unnatural movements."

The audience took their places in the auditorium. A fanfare of trumpets announced the arrival of the king. He took his place on his throne upon the raised dais in front of the stage. The curtain was drawn back to reveal a scene of hell with crimson burning fires. The audience gasped with horror at the sight. My moment had come. I stepped forward onto the stage and gave my speech:

> *"The owl is abroad, the bat, and the toad,*
> *And so is the cat-a-mountain,*
> *The ant and the mole sit both in a hole,*
> *And the frog peeps out o' the fountain;*
> *The dogs they do bay, and the timbrels play,*
> *The spindle is now a turning;*
> *The moon it is red, and the stars are fled,*
> *But all the sky is a-burning."*

A group of twelve masqued dancers dressed as witches emerged out of hell. They capered and whirled their way onto the stage. The dance was performed to the sound of infernal music. I saw the ladies in the audience recoil with horror. But the king leaned forward in his chair of estate and watched the performance intently. Suddenly, the music stopped and the witches vanished from sight. Then a magnificent House of Fame appeared filled with coloured lights that shone like emeralds, rubies and sapphires. It showed the hero Perseus and twelve masquers. They performed two ceremonial dances upon the stage and then formed the letters of Prince Charles' name. The king smiled graciously at this tribute and the audience applauded most enthusiastically.

Then came the queen's masque. The queen and her ladies represented idealised queens. Queen Anna wore a splendid gold collar set with jewels and pearls. The ladies performed a series of three ceremonial dances which ended in the figure of a diamond. They remained in that position while the musicians sang a song. The king was enchanted and called for them to be danced again. Afterwards, they partnered with gentlemen to perform galliards and corantoes. The evening concluded with a court revel and a banquet. The occasion was a great success and Master Jonson was deluged with compliments. He was sure that he would make his name and fortune from the queen's masques.

In April 1609 Lord Salisbury commissioned a masque from Master Jonson for the opening of the New Exchange in London. It was his new project to promote the trade of the city of London and he wanted to give it maximum publicity. The performance was called *"The Masque of the Key Keeper"* and it featured myself, Jack Underwood and William Ostler. I played the comic role of a shop-boy urging the customers to buy from his master:

"What do you lack? What is't you buy? Very fine China stuffs of all kinds and qualities? Caskets, umbrellas, sundials, hourglasses, looking-glasses, burning-glasses, crystal globes, waxen pictures, ostrich eggs and birds of paradise? Flowers of silk, mosaic fishes? Waxen fruit and porcelain dishes? Very fine cages for birds, billiard balls, purses, pipes, rattles, basins, ewers, cups, toothpicks, vizards, spectacles? Sir, what do you lack?"

The king and queen and their son Prince Henry attended the opening. Lord Salisbury presented the royal family with splendid gifts and distributed rings among the courtiers. Master Jonson was well satisfied for Lord Salisbury paid him thirteen pounds for his script. I was also satisfied for I received four pounds for performing in it. Afterwards I joined the throng of people inside the New Exchange. It was a shopping arcade on the Strand with two long galleries of shops. Master Jonson wandered off at once to peruse the bookshops. But I walked up and down admiring them all. They were luxury stores that sold imported silk, China porcelain and expensive manufactured goods. I thought what a fine thing it was to be a Londoner and see such wonders from abroad. Only wealthy gentlefolk could afford to purchase such costly merchandise. The milliner's shops sold beaver hats from North America to gentlemen of fashion. The draper's shops were full of ladies buying lawn cloth, silk stockings, cloth of gold, silver lace, coloured velvet and pearl ornaments. The mercer's shops sold exotic goods such as oranges, raisins, currants, pepper, sugar and tobacco. I stood close to the windows and feasted my eyes on the glorious sight. But they were far beyond my slender means. I would have to content myself with a pie and a bottle of ale from the hawkers.

How pleasant it must be to own such fine things, I thought. An actor wore elegant costumes on the stage, but it was only an illusion of life. We straddled two worlds; an imaginary world full of richness and drama and a real world fraught with poverty and hardship. Only a minority of players were successful enough to progress from survival to prosperity. I did not have the protection of a wealthy patron. But I had my talent and my determination to succeed. That would have to be enough.

Master Jonson broke my reverie. "Let us leave the gentlefolk to their pastimes and go back home to Blackfriars," he said. "We can stop at the

Mermaid on the way and share a good flask of wine together." I agreed. A glass of canary was the only real luxury that we could afford.

In the summer of 1609, the plague returned to the city of London, casting a dark shadow over its bustling streets. The playhouses were closed for fear of infection. It was a disaster for the companies. The King's Men lowered their flag at the Globe Theatre and locked its doors. Master Keysar was forced to take the company on a tour of the countryside. However, I resolved to stay in the city until the crisis passed. My mother sent me her receipt for a sure preventative. It consisted of half a handful each of angelica and celandine steeped in old ale. Others swore by the benefits of smoking pipe-tobacco. By late July, London was like a vast charnel house. The clergy urged their parishioners to repent for the end of the world was at hand. Red crosses were painted onto the doors of affected houses and the death-carts made the rounds every morning to collect the bodies of the dead. The bells of the parish churches did not cease to toll for the dead by day or night. Men walked down the streets with rue and wormwood stuffed into their nostrils and ears as a precaution against the pestilence. They looked for all the world like a boar's head at Christmas.

Since I could not act on the stage, I resolved to turn my hand to writing a play. It was a long-cherished ambition of mine to become a playwright. After all, I had performed in enough plays by now. And I had acted in enough bad plays to encourage me that I could do better if I took it up myself! I had read plenty of speeches and it would not be so hard to write my own. I had in mind a modern comedy of manners. I would call it: "*A Woman is a Weathercocke.*" It would be a satire on the subject of arranged marriages. There had recently been a great scandal at court over a pair of young aristocrats who had been forced into an unhappy match with tragic consequences. In 1606 Master Jonson had written the *"Masque of Hymen"* to celebrate the marriage of Robert Devereux, the earl of Essex, and Lady Frances Howard, the daughter of the earl of Suffolk. He was thirteen years old and she was fourteen. The match was a disaster and it ended in divorce.

Naturally, I could not write about this particular case but I knew that the audience would have it in their minds. I resolved that in my play the young ladies and their lovers would outwit the plans of their matchmaking father with a series of clever stratagems. I thought it was bound to be popular with the London crowds. I found the writing of my play a most welcome diversion from the miserable sights around me. It occupied me very pleasantly during the long months until the plague finally subsided. When the company returned to London, I brought my play to Master Keysar.

"I have written a new play," I announced with pride. "I pray that you will do me the honour of perusing it."

"Well done, Nat!" he replied. "I am always glad to read something new. Tell me what it is about."

"It is a romantic comedy set in London," I explained. "A man named Sir John Worldly has three daughters for whom he has arranged suitable marriages. But they are in love with other men. The three true suitors contrive ways to trick their rivals. By the end of the play, they have managed to win their ladies."

"It sounds just the thing to entertain the public," he said. "After this dreadful plague the people of London will be more than ready to enjoy a pleasant diversion."

When the theatres reopened, he gave me permission to put it on and we began the rehearsals. Robert Baxter played the role of the young hero Scudamore. But he constantly jumbled his words. I was convinced that he was doing it on purpose to spite me.

"You're fumbling it again!" I said irritably.

"It's not my fault, Nat," said Robert airily. "This page is so full of crossings out that I can hardly tell which lines to read."

"That's normal in a first draft," I snapped.

"Shakespeare's parts never have any corrections in them," he remarked. "He writes his lines perfectly at the first attempt."

"So, he claims!" I retorted, feeling nettled. "But I bet his desk is piled high with first drafts."

"I've seen him in action and it's quite true," he insisted. "But not every writer can be a genius like him, Nat."

"Take it again from the top," I said impatiently. "And this time, get it right. There are plenty of actors who can read their part perfectly the first time too. Your cue is:

"*In troth you were to blame to venture so. Mischiefs find us: we need not mischiefs seek.*"

Robert raised his eyebrows at me, but this time he read his speech flawlessly.

"*I am not tied to that opinion,
They are like women, which do always shun
Their lovers and pursuers, and do follow
With most rank appetites them that do fly:
All mischief that I had is but one woman,
And that one woman all mischance to me:*

Who speaks worst of them, there's the best of men.
They are like shadows: mischiefs are like them."

It was always Shakespeare whom the actors lauded. But for my part, I preferred the comedies of Master Jonson. London people and London life! That was what the playgoers wanted to see. Not these fusty tales of long ago or absurd fairy stories!

"People come to the theatre to be entertained," Maser Jonson said. "They want to watch comedies about everyday life. It is only the court that wants to see fantasies about classical myths or tragedies from ancient history. So, give the playgoers what they want!"

I heartily agreed with him. The reigning monarch had set the trend for too long in the theatre. Why should we write our plays to please them? I wanted to write about amusing contemporary subjects, not these grandiose dramas from long ago!

Finally, the rehearsals were over and the play was ready. I read the playbill with a great sense of pride and elation. *"Here within this place at three of the clock, shall be acted an excellent new comedy called A Woman is a Weathercocke by Nathan Field. Vivat Rex!"*

The play was well received by the playgoers and it was performed several times at Blackfriars over the next two months. At last, I had achieved my goal of putting on my own play! Now, I stood among my fellow playwrights as an equal. I was only twenty-two years old and I had already accomplished my first ambition. I vowed that this play would be the first of many more!

Master Jonson had also been hard at work during the barren plague season. He had written a new play called *"Epicene or The Silent Woman."*

"I have a fine part for you, Nat," he announced. "You shall play the role of Epicene. It is a boy who is disguised as a woman. A fine jest even if I say so myself!"

"What is the play about?" I enquired.

"It is a comedy," he said. "An elderly man named Morose decides to marry and disinherit his nephew, Dauphine. But he wants a silent woman for his wife as he cannot abide idle chatter. His barber introduces him to Epicene who seems to be the ideal choice. They get married, but she turns out to be a chatterbox whom he cannot abide. Then the nephew reveals that his wife is really a boy whom he has trained for the part."

I thought it was sure to please the playgoers. At the denouement, Dauphine snatched off my wig and turned to his uncle in triumph: "Here is your release, Sir!" he declared. "You have married a boy!"

The audience laughed at the revelation. But otherwise, the play was not well received. The gallants dubbed it "*The Silent Audience*" due to the lack of response it garnered. Master Jonson was disappointed by the reception of his play.

"It is quite impossible to please the playgoers," he complained. "They want bawdiness, satire and poetry to be combined in one play!"

In December 1609 our company performed three times during the Christmas festivities at court. The first play was "*Epicene*" by Master Jonson. The second play was "*The Knight of the Burning Pestle*" by my friend, Francis Beaumont. And to my delight, the third play was *A Woman is a Weathercocke*." Master Keysar was sufficiently impressed by that he had decided to take it to court. I felt a sweet pride in performing my own play at the palace. I had the pleasure of seeing the king and queen applaud my work. My cup was not just full, but running over! I looked forward to a future of even greater achievements. I was certain that one day I would be the greatest playwright in London and the most famous actor on the stage. My family would be proud of me in spite of their Puritan principles.

After the success of "*A Woman is a Weathercocke*" I gained a name for myself as a writer. I was invited to collaborate with other playwrights in producing new plays. Francis Beaumont and John Fletcher had devised an idea for a new play called "*The Maid's Tragedy.*" They asked me to join them one evening at The Mermaid tavern to plan out a rough draft of the plot. It was their favourite tavern since it stocked good canary wine. A bottle already stood on the table and John poured me a glass.

"This is no watered-down stuff, but your full Mermaid wine," he observed.

"What's this play about?" I asked them.

"It's a new idea," said Francis proudly. "The play is a revenge tragedy but it has scenes of romance in it. There have been plenty of romantic comedies before, but this will be a romantic tragedy."

"It is set in ancient Rhodes where General Amintor has just returned victorious from battle," explained Fletcher as he took a draught of ale. "He is engaged to marry the virtuous maid Aspatia. However, the king orders him to marry a lady named Evadne instead. On their wedding night she reveals that she is the king's mistress. The noble Amintor is appalled by this shameful revelation and thoughts of revenge stir within him. And that's as far as I've got with the script."

After a couple of hours of discussion and several glasses of canary, we had agreed upon the outline of the rest of the story. The ignoble king would be killed and then Evadne, Aspatia and Amintor would each tragically die in their turn. At the end of the play, a new king would take the throne and promise to rule honourably.

"I have a brilliant plot for how to kill the king," boasted Fletcher as he flourished his quill pen in the air. "You may safely leave that part to me!"

We split up the play between us according to our strengths. Fletcher took the tragic scenes; Beaumont took the love scenes and I undertook to write some of the dialogues.

The following morning, Fletcher was arrested on a charge of treason. His remark had been overheard by an informer and reported to the authorities. He was hauled off to Bridewell prison and clapped up as a felon. Then he was interrogated to make him divulge his murderous plot.

"I am a loyal subject of the king!" he protested. "I am a playwright. I was but discussing the plot of my latest play."

All of Fletchers friends rallied round and testified that he was indeed a well-known playwright in the London theatre and his character was blameless. Beaumont showed them the pages of *"The Maid's Tragedy"* and insisted that it was all a misunderstanding.

"Your informer is a fool!" he declared. "He has slandered the name of an honest man!"

Finally, the Lord Chamberlain intervened on his behalf and vouched for his innocence. Fletcher was released with a warning to be more careful about how he spoke of kings in the future. But he never lived it down. From that time on, he had to suffer jibes about being a dangerous fellow, a notorious scoundrel and gallows' bait. The play was completed, but after that incident, we were more circumspect in our choice of location for meetings. We realised that the Mermaid was a haunt of informers looking to earn themselves a bounty.

Master Jonson also invited me to collaborate with him on writing his court masques. He was busy with the script of his latest royal masque for Twelfth Night on 6th January 1610. This one was called "*The Lady of the Lake*" and it was performed in honour of Prince Henry. A masque was a flamboyant entertainment that combined singing, acting, music, dialogue, magnificent costumes and splendid scenery. Such was the demand for novelty that each one had to be more spectacular than the one before. He generously allowed me to write some of the actor's speeches. The masques included dances for the queen and her ladies to perform. They had become quite the fashion at court and they spent weeks rehearsing them with the Master of the Revels. The masques had received much praise. But Master Jonson was concerned that the elaborate sets received more attention than his well-written speeches in praise of the monarchy.

"What about your plays, Master Jonson?" I asked him. "Have you given them up?"

"Not entirely," he replied. "But at this season, masques are all the vogue."

"Plays can be as successful as masques," I insisted. It troubled me that he was neglecting the theatre for the court.

"What did you get for "*Weathercocke*," Nat?" he enquired.

"Forty shillings," I replied.

"Exactly! A few paltry shillings in return for many months of labour. Not one play in five makes much of a profit. I have made less than two hundred pounds from all of my plays. These court masques pay far better. I get forty pounds every time. It stands to reason that a queen can afford to pay more than any London stage manager," he declared.

"But Shakespeare did well enough," I persisted.

"Ha!" he retorted. "The poet Edmund Spencer wrote *"The Faerie Queen"* in praise of Elizabeth I and he was rewarded with a pension for life. Fifty pounds a year for one poem! That is the best course for a writer, Nat. Find yourself a lordly patron who can afford to maintain you. That is the prize!"

Master Jonson was always a shrewd operator. He had moved from being a freelance playwright to the foremost writer of masques. He had managed to corner the market on writing the Christmas court masques in partnership with the stage designer Inigo Jones. The other playwrights grumbled that they never got their turn.

"It's a sure thing, Nat," he continued with satisfaction. "I always get a handsome fee for my services. And I don't have to worry about whether it will be a success or flop with the playgoers. Furthermore, it leads to other commissions from nobles of the court. It's a regular goldmine and I intend to keep on profiting from it."

In the summer of 1610, word of a new scandal enlivened the country. Lady Arbella Stuart was arrested for having married William Seymour, Lord Beauchamps, without permission from the king. She was detained in the house of Sir Thomas Perry in Lambeth and he was sent to the Tower. Remarkably, she managed to arrange their escape from captivity. When news of their escape became public it caused a great sensation. The Privy Council offered great rewards in return for information about their whereabouts. The citizens of London awaited the outcome with bated breath and it became the favourite topic for discussion in the taverns. I admired her courage and hoped that the couple would reach safety in Europe. But Master Jonson was doubtful of such a happy resolution.

"Lady Arbella should have satisfied herself with living the life of a great noblewoman," he observed. "At least King James was prepared to receive her at court which was more than Queen Elizabeth I was willing to do. But he can't allow them to slip through his fingers in this way. They are not only claimants, but Catholic claimants. Either France or Spain could use them to spearhead an invasion. It would be better for everyone if they were recaptured!"

Finally, the drama reached its climax. Lord Beauchamps fled to Ostend while Lady Arbella set sail for Calais. But her ship was overtaken in the Channel and she was brought back to England. She was imprisoned in the Tower and never saw her husband again. I remembered how she had taken such delight in our performances at Hardwick Hall. I felt sorry that so fine a lady should end her days as an unhappy prisoner. Her only crime was seeking to take a husband. It was a tragic outcome for someone who might have succeeded Queen Elizabeth I on the throne.

The queen's next commission for Master Jonson was the "*Masque of Love*." It was presented at court on 3rd February 1611. It never failed to delight me to receive an invitation to perform at court. Very few commoners ever had the chance to visit a royal palace. I was now well known to Sir George Buck, the new Master of the Revels. I looked forward eagerly to seeing my latest costume. It was another lavish creation made of embroidered silk and silver lace which had been made with no regard for the expense. It was worth a fortune and I wished that I could keep it. But I suspected that Sir George Buck was becoming rich by claiming the costumes as his perquisites and selling them to the dealers. Master Jonson confided to me that each masque cost five thousand pounds to produce. I was staggered to hear that so much money was thrown away on a single night's entertainment. But he assured me that making such an extravagant display was the entire purpose of the occasion.

"It is expected of the monarchy," he explained. "It is the tradition to stage these elaborate spectacles which inspire awe in the onlookers. It demonstrates the glory of the court and the majesty of the king to the rest of the world."

Master Jonson had prepared an anti-masque which featured twelve She-Follies and a dance of twelve musicians. In the queen's masque, Queen Anna appeared as the Queen of the Orient and her ladies represented the daughters of the Morning. I appeared as the figure of Love bound in chains and appealed to the ladies to rescue me:

> "Ladies, have your looks no power
> To help Love at such an hour?
> Will you lose him thus? adieu,
> Think, what will become of you,
> Who shall praise you, who admire,
> Who shall whisper, by the Fire
> As you stand, soft tales; who bring you
> Pretty News, in Rimes who sing you,
> Who shall bathe him in the streams
> Of your blood, and send you dreams
> Of delight."

The queen and her ladies performed their dances before the king and his court. I made the final speech of Love to signal the end of the masque:

> "Now, Gentle Love is free, and Beauty blest
> With the sight it so much long'd to see.
> Let us the Muses Priests, and Graces go to rest,
> For in them our labours happy be.

Then, then, angry Musick sound, and teach our feet,
How to move in time, and measure meet:
Thus should the Muses Priests, and Graces go to rest
Bowing to the Sun, throned in the West."

Finally, the masque was concluded and the courtiers took their partners to dance in the revels. I enjoyed watching them showing off their dancing skills and vying for the king's attention. They wore their newest garments and flaunted themselves like a flock of peacocks on the green. The gentlemen were even vainer than the ladies of the court. Perhaps they thought they had more to gain by making a fine display. After all, Robert Carr had nothing to recommend him but his looks and now he was a Gentlemen of the Bedchamber. Master Jonson came to join me. I expected him to be in great spirits at the success of his latest production. But he seemed strangely downcast.

"Everyone is full of compliments about the costumes, the dancing and the scenery," he grumbled. "But these things are only the gaudy outward feathers. They do not realise that it is the poetry that lies at the very heart of the masque. The king and his court are only interested in watching a grand spectacle. I do not get my due as the composer of the verse and the mastermind of the occasion. It is no season for a writer to make his name as a court poet!"

CHAPTER 11

The Lady Elizabeth's Men

*"Our Scene is London, 'cause we would make known,
No country's mirth is better than our own.
No clime breeds better matter, for your whore,
Bawd, squire, imposter, many persons more"*

(The Alchemist, Ben Jonson, 1610).

In 1611 I completed my second play which was called *"Amends for Ladies."* It was another city comedy in which the husband of Lady Perfect set out to test her chastity. She passed the test with flying colours and he was forced to beg her forgiveness. It was an amusing piece and I had high hopes for its success. The play began with a comic dialogue in which a maid, a wife and a widow debated which one of them has the better lot in life. But when it was performed, it was not as well received as *"A Woman is a Weathercocke."* In my disappointment, I thought about giving up on writing plays. But Master Fletcher wouldn't hear of it.

"Not every play is a success, Nat," he consoled me. "But rather than writing your own plays, you should collaborate with others. It means a finished play in less than half the time and labour. Believe me, collaboration is the future of playwriting."

"Have you got any ideas?" I asked him.

"Yes, a play called *"The Honest Man's Fortune."* The hero is called Montaigne and he is persecuted by the jealous duke of Orleans. He wrongly suspects that his wife is being unfaithful with him and contrives his ruin. Montaigne takes service in the house of a virtuous lady named Lamira. Finally, his fortunes are restored and he defeats his rival suitors to marry her."

We completed the play together and I played the leading role of the honest man, Montaigne. I found that portraying the male lead was much more to my taste than playing the female roles. I had the looks of a young hero and I could dress and act the part of a romantic gallant with great conviction. The audience applauded my performance and I contributed a great deal to the success of the play. Master Fletcher congratulated me on bringing his creation to life so memorably. I looked forward to creating many more roles in the future.

Our next collaboration was a play called *"The Triumph of Honour."* Sophocles, the duke of Athens, is defeated in battle by the Roman general Martius. He refuses to plead for his life but his noble wife Dorigen successfully intercedes for mercy. Martius falls in love with her, but she resists him and offers to stab herself to death. He is shamed into repentance saying, *"Live, live, thou angel of thy sex."* Her matchless courage and honour saved both her husband and her virtue. The audience were delighted by the happy ending and we received much praise.

Shortly afterwards, the company performed *"The Coxcomb"* by Beaumont and Fletcher. This was a comedy about a traveller named Mercury who falls in love with the beautiful wife of his friend Antonio. The absurd humour of the play very much appealed to the playgoers of London. By now, the two writers were such good friends that they had moved into shared lodgings together near the theatre. However, they were often to be found writing their scenes at the Mermaid tavern. They claimed that the convivial atmosphere gave them greater inspiration. But I suspected it had more to do with the excellent wine.

In January 1612 I appeared in the *"Masque of Love Restored."* I played the role of Love as I had done before. The masque commenced with a comic interlude of Robin Goodfellow who sweeps the hearth while the maids are at play. Then I entered and made my speech dressed in the garb of Cupid bearing my golden bow and arrow.

"O, how came Love, that is himself a fire,
To be so cold?
Yes, tyrant Money quencheth all desire,
Or makes it old.
But here are beauties will revive
Love's youth, and keep his heat alive:
As often as his torch here dies,
He needs but light it at fresh eyes.
Joy, joy, the more: for in all courts,
If love be cold, so are his sports."

The queen and her ladies performed their ceremonial dances and then several gentlemen of the court approached to partner them in a galliard. But at the last minute, Lady Frances Howard and her sister Catherine Howard flatly refused to dance with their partners. Apparently, they considered them too far below them in rank. So, the unfortunate men were forced to partner each other instead. The court regarded their predicament as most amusing.

That summer, Master Jonson took me to visit his friend Raleigh in the Tower. Their friendship had weathered many storms, but this was a tempest unlike any other. The dim light of the cell cast elongated shadows on the cold stone walls. As Master Jonson stepped inside, his eyes met Raleigh's. The lines etched upon his face told a story of loss and regret. He had once been a celebrated warrior and explorer, a leading light of the court. But now his vibrant spirit had dulled, like a blade worn out by years of battles. His hands, once calloused from gripping a sword hilt, now rested on the worn flagstones. I watched him from the corner, my heart heavy with sympathy.

"Good day to you, Sir Walter," said Master Jonson. "I trust my visit has not come at an inconvenient time?" His gaze lingered on Raleigh's dishevelled hair, once neatly combed for royal audiences.

Raleigh gave a painful smile. "Time is all the riches that I have now," he replied. "I am free to spend it abundantly." His fingers traced invisible patterns on the stone, as if seeking solace in its rough texture.

"How is your *magnum opus* progressing?" he enquired sympathetically. In his confinement Raleigh had undertaken to write "*The History of the World.*" The cell contained a large table set with an inkstand and a pile of parchment. The window ledge displayed a row of volumes and the walls of the cell were hung with a variety of maps drawn in coloured inks.

Raleigh sat up straighter at the mention of his project. "I have already undertaken the discourse of the first kings and kingdoms," he replied proudly. "I shall now proceed to relate the stories of the kings of England down to King Henry VIII. It is time that his tale was told honestly. If all the knowledge of merciless princes was lost to the world, it might be painted again out of the life of this king."

"That is a bold endeavour," replied Master Jonson, raising his eyebrows. "None of the previous chroniclers have dared to name his faults."

"There is no lack of them," he replied defiantly. "How many servants did he advance and then ruin again with the change of his fancy? How many wives did he cast off as his affection altered? How many princes of the blood did he execute? But beside all these sorrows, he consumed more treasure than all our victorious kings in their wars of conquest. It is the duty of the historian to hold him up for censure. His example will serve as a warning to his successors to rule justly and be remembered for their virtues." I thought that Raleigh was playing a dangerous game in writing his history. King James would not take kindly to being instructed by a mere subject.

But Master Jonson made no objection to his plan. "I shall see to its publication as soon as the work is complete," he promised. "Is there any other service I can offer you?"

"I am concerned for the future of my son Wat," he replied. "In my confinement, I cannot do for him what a father should. Will you take him on a tour of Europe? I can think of no-one better to be his tutor."

"I would be honoured," said Master Jonson. "A visit to the Continent is a fine venture for a young man. It is the best way for him to learn foreign languages and gain a greater degree of polish and sophistication."

At one time, Raleigh could have brought his son to court. He would have found him a good office and made him a worthy marriage among the leading houses of the kingdom. Young Wat would have inherited his father's estate and his fortune would have been assured. But now the family estate had been forfeited to the crown and his future was uncertain. He was the son of a once-great man whose name was now stained with the taint of treason. He would never escape the taunts of his father's enemies. It was by far the best solution for him to travel abroad. And so, Master Jonson and Wat Raleigh set out on a tour of France and the Netherlands. I envied them the opportunity to travel abroad. I would have loved to visit the playhouses of France for it was said that they employed female actresses on the stage. But I had far too many commitments to be able to leave London.

In 1612 my friends Beaumont and Fletcher wrote their first tragicomedy together called "*Philaster*." It told the story of Prince Philaster of Sicily whose throne had been usurped by the king of Calabria. He planned to marry his daughter to a Spanish prince in order to deprive Philaster of his claim to the kingdom. I could play a graceful lady on the stage, but I made a devastatingly handsome young gallant. In performing the role of the heroic Philaster I knew that I had created a masterpiece. The playgoers never failed to weep when I was sentenced to death. They rejoiced when I was finally restored to my crown. I experienced the power of a true artist to move people by the sheer mastery of my art. The play was a great success and I basked in the admiration of the crowd. My friends took me off in triumph to celebrate at the Mermaid. There they toasted me as a prince among actors.

The play was performed in court to equal acclaim. The noble audience listened attentively and applauded me with enthusiasm. Some of the ladies were moved to tears which they concealed behind their jewelled fans. But more importantly, the play succeeded in pleasing both the king and the queen. Sir George Buck took me to make my bow before them.

"Here is the noble Philaster, your Majesties," he announced. "I think you will agree that he is the very model of a virtuous prince."

"Aye, so he is," agreed King James, nodding his head vigorously. "It pleases us to see upright conduct receive its due reward. We would see more of such plays performed at our court. Is that not so, my dear?"

"You are quite right, your Grace," the queen emphatically agreed. "It was as good as listening to a sermon only it was far more entertaining. It is just what we wish for the good instruction of our court."

I made a graceful bow before them. "As the moon is eclipsed by the sun, so the modest virtues of Philaster are far outshone by your Majesties."

King James looked gratified by the compliment and reached for his purse. I was confident of receiving a generous recompense. My head teamed with wonderful thoughts: *This could be the first step to gaining royal favour and preferment at court. In time I could become a respected courtier or even a knight*. But at that very moment, the king's favourite came over to join us. He was now known as Viscount Rochester. He was dressed in a doublet and hose of blue velvet embroidered with gold thread which set off his fair hair. Around his neck he wore a heavy gold chain set with sapphires. He stood beside the king's chair of estate and looked me up and down with open disdain.

"He is quite talented for a common player," he remarked spitefully.

The king's demeanour changed at his derisive tone. He looked abashed and withdrew his hand from his purse. Then he pursed his lips and frowned. "It is time for us to dine," he announced and waved his fingers in dismissal. Viscount Rochester smirked at my look of dismay. The audience was over and my golden hopes of reward were lost. Sir George Buck promptly led me away from the king's presence. "Viscount Rochester is jealous of the king's attention," he whispered to me. "He lives in fear of losing his favour to a rival." I was well aware that the court was a nest of venomous snakes. But I was downcast at how quickly my triumph had turned into dust. I reminded myself that I still had the favour of the London crowds. Even if the king and his favourite disregarded me, I would still make my fame and fortune on the public stage.

Beaumont and Fletcher followed up their achievement by writing the tragedy of *"Cupid's Revenge."* In this play, Leontius, the duke of Lycia, outlawed the worship of the god Cupid in his domain. In revenge, Cupid brought about the ruin and death of the royal family by means of fatal romances. I cut a splendid figure as the tragic Leontius and the audience adored me. It was another popular success which further enhanced my name as a leading actor and my friend's reputations as up-and-coming playwrights.

In the autumn, Master Jonson returned to London again. I met him down at the Mermaid tavern. "How was your trip?" I asked him. I was eager to hear of his adventures abroad.

He groaned. "Never again shall I be so ill-advised as to accompany a young sprig on a tour of the Continent! That boy is a rogue! He led me many a merry dance, I can tell you. It was more than my nerves could stand for I was responsible for his well-being. What could I have said to his father if he had come to any harm?"

"And did it?" I prompted him.

"He did not, but it was another story with me. On one occasion he got me drunk, put me in a wheelbarrow and rolled me through the streets of Paris for all to see! I was only too glad to return to England and discharge him off my hands. No doubt he is already creating havoc with his friends again but thankfully it is no concern of mine."

It amused me to hear of young Wat's exploits. Only a young nobleman could afford to run riot in that way. A commoner's son would soon find themselves behind bars if they dared to make any trouble for the authorities.

In November 1612, Prince Henry died suddenly from typhoid fever. He was only eighteen years old and had been regarded as a youth of great promise. The news of his death cast a gloom over London and he was greatly mourned. He had been far more popular than his father.

"He is a great loss to the nation," said Master Jonson regretfully. "He would have made a far better monarch than King James. He had every quality that his father lacked. He was charismatic, intelligent and athletic. He would have restored the prestige of the monarchy. I shall compose a eulogy in his honour."

The heir to the throne was now his younger brother, Charles Stuart. Nothing was known about him except that he was a sickly boy. Queen Anna was distraught at the loss of her beloved son. She lost interest in planning any new court masques and left their devising to others.

In February 1613 Princess Elizabeth married Prince Frederick V of the Palatinate. The wedding took place in the Chapel Royal of Whitehall Palace. Afterwards a masque was presented in the Banqueting House. It was called the *Masque of Lords and Honourable Maids*. The masque was devised by Thomas Campion and Inigo Jones. The Master of the Revels commissioned our company to perform in the masque. This time we were dressed as stars and placed upon moving clouds. Solomon Pavy sang a song imploring the stars to come down to earth:

> *"Large grow their beams, their near approach afford them so*
> *By nature, sights that pleasing are, cannot too amply show;*
> *Oh, might these flames in human shapes descend to grace this place,*
> *How lovely would their presence be, their forms how full of grace!"*

Sixteen torchbearers danced below and invited the bride and bridegroom come onto the stage and dance with them. Princess Elizabeth wore a dress of cloth of silver adorned with diamonds and a jewelled crown. The bridegroom wore a doublet and hose of white satin set with pearls. I thought the masque was very beautiful, but naturally Master

Jonson dismissed it as a very inferior concept. "All the reports I have heard from the court assure me that it was of no great commendation," he remarked. At the end of April, they set sail for Ostend accompanied by a retinue of over six hundred people. Inigo Jones was included in the entourage for the princess had commissioned him to build an indoor theatre in her new home at Heidelberg Castle.

At the end of June 1613, Master Jonson and I went to visit the Globe theatre. It was showing a new play called *"All is True"* by William Shakespeare. It was based on the life of King Henry VIII. It was a bold subject for him to have chosen and we were curious to see how he had dramatized it.

"He'd never have dared to write it during the reign of Queen Elizabeth," observed Master Jonson. "But I'm surprised that he got it past the censors even now. King James thinks that monarchs are the breathing images of God upon earth. I wouldn't have thought he would approve of it."

I wore my best doublet and hose of goose-turd green velvet for the excursion. It was an idyllic summer's day with a clear blue sky overhead. It was perfect for idling the afternoon away at the playhouse. In this season, the path beside the river Thames was not clogged with thick black mud. It ought to have been verdant with grass, but the blazing heat had dried the blades into dry stalks which crunched beneath our feet. The familiar white bulk of the Globe came into view and we quickened our steps. Its pennant flag was flying prominently overhead to signal that a play would be shown that day.

The new play was popular and great crowds of playgoers streamed through the doors into the playhouse. We elbowed our way towards the front of the yard. The play set out to present a fine spectacle of the royal court to the audience. The players were splendidly costumed as royal guards in their embroidered coats and knights of the order with their Georges and Garter. The groundlings cheered as Dick Burbage appeared wearing the red vestments of Cardinal Wolsey. He welcomed a company of ladies to attend a masque at his palace of York Place on the river Thames. Then a barge arrived carrying Henry VIII and a group of courtiers. A cannon fired to salute the arrival of the king. That was the mischief for a spark landed on the thatched roof of the playhouse and began to kindle. But the eyes of the audience were too bent upon the stage to notice that anything was amiss. The scene portrayed the fateful meeting between King Henry and Mistress Anne Boleyn. The musicians began to play for a revel. They dance with each other and the king is overwhelmed by her grace and charm:

"The fairest hand I ever touch'd! O beauty,
Till now I never knew thee!" he declared.

"He's playing it safe, sticking to the pageantry," Master Jonson muttered. I shrugged. Everyone knew the tragic story of Henry VIII and Anne Boleyn. The novelty lay in seeing old King Henry portrayed on the stage at all. Smoke began to rise from the thatch, but the playgoers paid no attention. They watched with baited breath as the king kissed her. The company exited the stage to attend a banquet. The playgoers turned and chattered to each other in anticipation of the next scene. Suddenly a shout went up: "Look the roof is on fire!"

By now the fire had taken hold in the thatched roof and spread in both directions around the ring of the Globe theatre. It crackled and burned as it devoured the dry straw and the underlying timbers. People began to panic. They pushed and shoved their way towards the two narrow exits. Master Jonson and I feared that we would be crushed or trampled in the rush to get out of the theatre. The flames ran down the beams to ground level and clouds of smoke filled the air all around us. The playgoers were so distracted that a number of them left their cloaks behind them as they fled. One man started screaming that his breeches were on fire. That might have been disastrous if his neighbour had not quickly doused him with the bottle of beer in his hand. Finally, we fought our way out of the exit into the safety of the fresh air. We stood back and watched the spectacle of the great playhouse going up in flames. Plumes of smoke were rising from the Bankside into the sky. Suddenly a woman started shrieking:

"My child! My child is still inside! Somebody take pity and save him!"

A courageous man ran back into the smoke-filled entrance of the building. We waited anxiously for his return. Suddenly he reappeared clutching a small boy to his chest. His clothes were smouldering from the heat and he was coughing fit to burst from the smoke. A cheer went up. The crowd surrounded him and tore off his smouldering clothes. Then he was taken away to a nearby house to have his burns treated. By now, the news of the disaster had spread far and wide and great crowds accumulated all around us. It seemed that half of London was gathered at the scene. We stood and gazed in awe at the sight of the blazing thatch and timbers. The Globe was already like a great bonfire. There was no hope of saving it. Smoke and ashes billowed around us making us cough. Great smuts landed on our faces and clothes and grey dust powdered our hair. But nobody budged from their place. It was like watching a vision of the Last Days. I could well imagine what the Puritan preachers would be telling their congregations.

"How did it happen?" I heard the newcomers asking the playgoers.

"I heard 'twas a cannon set it off!" one man replied, his eyes glued to the conflagration.

"Aye, a stagehand fired a cannon to announce the arrival of the king," said another. "And a spark set light to the thatched roof. He wasn't quick enough to put it out and the fire took hold and spread. It went up so fast that it was a miracle that nobody died. But the whole theatre is lost!"

Indeed, it was well and truly gone. We watched the great edifice slowly sink into ruins in front of us. I felt sorry for the King's Men. They had lost their theatre and their livelihood. But it was good news for the other playhouses for now all the playgoers would come to us instead. Master Jonson and I headed for the Mermaid tavern to quench our thirst. But all of the taverns were filled to bursting. Ashes were still falling from the sky and my eyes were smarting. So, we made our way back to Blackfriars to change our clothes.

"It was a fire worthy of the wrath of Vulcan!" observed Master Jonson. "It may inspire me to pen a verse or two in its memory. So fine a playhouse deserves a tribute!"

The rest of the players were astounded when I arrived looking like a soul in torment. They cursed their ill-fortune at missing the spectacle. My best doublet was completely ruined and I had no choice but to throw it away. Master Keysar was remarkably sanguine when he heard the news.

"Well, it is just their ill-fortune," he remarked. "Every business has its hazards. They ought to have kept sandbags or a bucket of water by the cannon."

"What do you think they will do?" I asked.

"Master Heminges is not short of a few crowns," he observed. "He and the other shareholders can well afford to rebuild the Globe again. In the meantime, they will have to rent another playhouse or else go out touring. I wouldn't be surprised if he doesn't come making enquiries here. Well, I shall be willing to hear any proposal he may wish to make."

By 1613 Master Keysar had grown tired of the poor returns of theatre management. He returned the lease on the Blackfriars theatre to Master Burbage. He promptly turned it over to the use of his own company, the *King's Men,* and they used it both winter and summer until the Globe was rebuilt. They obtained not only the lease of the theatre but also the cat Felix. He had grown from a scrawny kitten into a splendid creature with a magnificent coat and a fluffy tail. He was now a regular fixture and a favourite of the patrons.

Our company merged with the *Lady Elizabeth's Men* which was managed by Master Philip Henslowe. He owned the Hope playhouse and knew everything about the world of the theatre. Now I was part of a company of adult players. But I still performed as a leading actor. Our first performance was a new comedy called *"A Chaste Maid in Cheapside"* by Thomas Middleton. However, the new company was not as successful as the *"Children of the Revels"* had been. I was arrested for debt several times and had to appeal to Master Henslowe for a loan. He was always forthcoming for he could hardly stage his plays without me.

In October 1614 Master Johnson wrote a new play for our company called *"Bartholomew Fair."* I played the leading role of John Littlewit who invited his friends to the fair to watch a puppet show. But once at the fair they all fell prey to a variety of misadventures. The play was a success and I expected Master Jonson to be delighted. But he was irritated by the remarks that it was too commonplace a subject. "The multitude do not come for what is right and proper, they prefer the unreasonable or impossible," he complained.

After this we performed *"The Scornful Lady"* by Beaumont and Fletcher. At the start of the play, Elder Loveless, has offended his lady by forcing her to kiss him in public. He asks her forgiveness and urges her to marry him. But she insists that he must travel abroad for a year as a penance. He leaves his house and income to the care of his dissolute younger brother Young Loveless. But then he returns in disguise in order to test the faithfulness of his brother and his lady. The play turned out to be their most successful comedy. But my aim was set higher than a career in a minor company. In 1614 the Globe theatre reopened again. It had a tiled roof in place of its thatch and was regarded as the fairest theatre in the kingdom.

In January 1615 a new masque was presented at the court called *"The Vision of Delight"*. There must have been at least a thousand lords and ladies present for the occasion. The ladies were dressed as richly as queens in gowns and mantles of many colours. They wore strings of jewels around their necks and in their girdles which glittered like stars in the dim light of the hall. On their heads were delicate plumes and, in their hands, they carried plumed fans. *"The Vision of Delight"* was a masque about dreams in which the performers were presented as dream figures appearing in the night. The dream world was ruled by the figure of Phantasy, who called forth different species of dreams. I gave the opening speech to the honourable audience:

"Break, Fantasy, from thy cave of cloud
And spread thy purple wings;
Now all thy figures are allowed,
And various shapes of things;
Create of airy forms a stream;
It must have blood and nought of phlegm,
And though it be a waking dream,
Yet let it like an odour rise
To all the senses here,
And fall like sleep upon their eyes,
Or music in their ear."

The antimasque featured amusing but insignificant "*Phantasms*." Then the golden-haired Hour appeared to celebrate the coming of the New Year. Finally, King James was presented as the universal king who brought peace and harmony to the world. Naturally, this went over very well.

"'Tis he, 'tis he, and no power else,
That makes all this what phantasy tells;
The founts, the flowers, the birds, the bees,
The heards, the flocks, the grasse, the trees,
Do all confesse him; but most These
Who call him lord of the foure seas,
King of the lesser and greater isles,
And all those happy when he smiles.
Advance, his favour calls you to advance,
And do your homage in a dance."

This was the signal for the revels to begin. Most of the courtiers seized the opportunity to take part in the dancing. But I noticed that a group of people were gathered before the king's dais. I drew closer and overheard Lord Somerset, the Lord Chamberlain, making the introductions:

"Your Majesty, I have the honour to present Master John Rolfe and his wife, Princess Pocahontas, from Virginia in the New World!"

The couple made their obeisances to his Majesty. I thought he was a rather plain-looking man, but she was a beautiful woman with brown skin, dark eyes and a dignified expression. They were both dressed in fashionable court clothes which demonstrated how well their lives had prospered over in the new colony.

"Welcome to my court, Master Rolfe," replied the king. "I hear you are the first man of Virginia to marry a lady of the New World. How did it come about?"

"I arrived at Jamestown in 1510, your Majesty," he explained. "Times were very hard for the early settlers. One of the bravest men, named John Smith, went out exploring the territory. He was captured by a native hunting party. They brought him before their chief Powhatan and drew their clubs to beat out his brains. He would have died if it were not for the intervention of my wife, Pocahontas. She was the favourite child of the chief and rescued the captive by taking his head in her arms." He paused dramatically. The king was fascinated by the adventurous tale.

"Go on man, go on!" he urged him. I was equally enthralled by the story and thought it would make a marvellous play. By now, a large crowd had gathered around us. Master Rolfe smiled and resumed his story.

"Afterwards, she persuaded her father to have him conducted safely back to Jamestown. She befriended the colonists and made visits to our settlement. She brought provisions to us when we were starving and saved many lives. Our minister taught her to speak English and she became a Christian. My own wife had died during the voyage and so I asked permission of the governor to marry her." I thought Master Rolfe had made a great success of his audience. King James was leaning forward in his chair and listening with the utmost attention.

"She is a most courageous lady," he said approvingly. "And how do you support yourself in the colonies. Do you hunt or trap the wild beasts there?" His eyes lit up with enthusiasm. I thought that Master Rolfe was about to captivate the king with stories of his hunting prowess in the New World. Unfortunately, he had not been forewarned about the king's tastes. His answer destroyed his opportunity of gaining favour.

"I am a farmer, your Majesty," he replied. "I own a plantation named Varina Farms and I make my living by cultivating the new crop of tobacco. I have brought a great cargo of it here to England."

Instantly, the king's expression changed. He was a strong opponent of the new fashion of smoking. "I am sorry to hear it, Master Rolfe. It is a noxious weed and I have banned it from my court!"

The Lord Chamberlain quickly ushered the pair away from the king's presence. They left the Banqueting Hall immediately and I was disappointed not to have the opportunity of making their acquaintance. I would have liked to have heard more about their life in Virginia. If only Master Rolfe had answered with more discretion his sensational story would have upstaged the success of the queen's masque. It was so easy to make a blunder at court, especially with so mercurial a man as King James. It only took one simple mistake and you had ruined your chances for good. But the remarkable story of Pocahontas quickly spread around the court. Master Johnson was most struck by it. I could see that he was already contemplating the idea of a masque about the New World.

CHAPTER 12

The King's Men

"All the world's a stage."

("As You Like It:" Act 2 Scene 7)
(The motto inscribed upon the flag of the Globe theatre in London).

"Players have many excellent qualities: as dancing, music, song, elocution, ability of body, memory, skill of weapon, pregnancy of wit and such like"

(Thomas Gainesford, The Rich Cabinet, 1616).

In 1616 my friend Jack Underwood came to see me. "Master Shakespeare has sold his share in the Globe and retired to Stratford," he said. "It leaves a vacancy in the King's Men. You should think about it, Nat." I didn't have to think about it. Being a member of the King's Men was a great accolade for a player.

"How do I let them know that I'm interested?" I asked him.

"I'll let them know," he replied with a wink. He was as good as his word. A few weeks later I was invited to meet the great Richard Burbage. He was short and stout man with a dominating presence.

"So boy, you want to be a player at the Globe?" he challenged me.

"Yes, if you please Master Burbage," I replied eagerly.

"Such a well-mannered boy," he remarked sardonically. "Are you sure you want to live the life of a vagabond?"

"I would like nothing better," I insisted.

"Well, we shall see, Master Field," he replied. "Take this part and read it over. Then I shall hear you perform. Here at the Globe, we present comedies, histories, and tragedies. The players act all the dramatic roles as required. We do not confine ourselves to satiric city-comedies."

I took the page and scanned it rapidly. It was a speech by a lady lamenting her faithless lover. My heart sank to my boots. I would much rather have played the role of the hero. But if he wanted to test my versatility, that was all the same to me. Perhaps he wanted to see if I could partner with him in romantic love scenes. I made my voice as soft and sweet as possible as I recited the words:

"Let me go, farewell, I must from hence,
These words are poyson to poore Didos soule,
O speake like my Aeneas, like my love:
Why look'st thou toward the sea? the time hath been
When Didos beautie chaind thine eyes to her:
Am I lesse faire then when thou sawest me first?
O then Aeneas, tis for griefe of thee:
Say thou wilt stay in Carthage with thy Queene,
And Didos beautie will returne againe:
Aeneas, say, how canst thou take thy leave?
Wilt thou kisse Dido? O thy lips have sworne
To stay with Dido: canst thou take her hand?

Thy hand and mine have plighted mutual faith,
Therefore unkind Aeneas, must thou say,
Then let me goe, and never say farewell?"

"And so, Dido, Queen of Carthage laments the departure of her lover Aeneus," observed Master Burgage. "You have a passable voice for declamation. But where is the depth of emotion in the words, the black despair suffered for a lost love? Of course, you are too young to have had a lover. You will have to imagine what you have not yet experienced. Then you will gain the power to thrill an audience. Can you sing, boy?"

"Yes, Master Burbage," I said confidently.

"He waved his hand. "Go ahead and entertain me, Master Field."

I thought quickly. I sang a song from the last court revel and followed it with a dance sequence. Silence followed. Master Burbage observed me with a frown. "Well enough, boy. But here we do not entertain queens, but commoners. What pleases them most is a clever clown who can tease their wits. But that I can teach you."

And so, I joined the company of the King's Men. The Globe was the biggest theatre in London. Master Burbage was its star attraction, but there were other leading lights in the company. I would have to prove myself to them. But I had no doubt of my talents. I had always out-classed my fellow players from the beginning. Jack made me welcome on my arrival and the other players seemed pleased that I had joined them. The Globe theatre was a far more ambitious enterprise than Blackfriars and it was lavishly resourced. The tiring house contained a splendid collection of costumes. The company purchased them from the servants of noblemen. They would often be given cast-off clothing by their masters. But since they were too fine for them to wear, they would sell them to the playhouses. The manager had fresh backdrops painted for every new performance. Whenever I had the chance, I watched the other actors perform and noted their tricks. Some had a marvellous gift of comedy and repartee with the crowds. Others preferred to emphasise their gift of dramatic storytelling. I made a special play of my skills at singing and dancing. Naturally, I was teased as the pretty little chorister, but I took no heed of it.

In fact, I wasn't needed to play the female roles. The company had younger boy actors for those parts. As a young man I was generally cast as the second lead. Master Burbage played the leading male roles and the tragic heroes. He had played the title roles in Henry V, Hamlet, Othello and King Lear. I would often partner with him in scenes. The first play in which I performed at the Globe was *"Macbeth"* by Master Shakespeare. Burbage played the role of the ambitious general Macbeth and I played his friend Banquo. It told the story of the murder of an ancient king of Scotland and how his untimely death had led to terrible consequences. The play had been written to please King James and it featured a trio of witches. I was proud to have realised my ambition of performing onstage with Master Burbage. I was overwhelmed by the power of his performances which drew all eyes towards him.

"What's the secret?" I asked him one day.

"Acting is not just a matter of dressing the part and declaiming the lines of the play, Nat."

"What do you mean?"

"You have to forget what your teachers told you," he said, wagging his finger. "None of them know anything. How could they? They have never performed all the great roles on the stage. Acting is far more than declaiming your speeches and matching them to the right gestures. You have to enter into the character and understand them. You think like them, stand like them, walk like them. Finally, you become the character. Only then will you give a true performance that will move people."

I was intrigued by this new possibility and observed his performances more closely. He did become the characters he played and his performances were convincing. I started giving more thought to my characters so that they weren't just stereotyped heroes, villains and clowns. I was determined to outdo Master Burbage and our relationship on the stage became a friendly rivalry. We partnered together in a series of plays including *"The Alchemist," "Volpone," "The Queen of Corinth"* and *"The Knight of Malta."* He was the king of the stage, but I was the prince. I was determined that one day I would be the leading actor of the company. Master Shakespeare had written many leading roles with Master Burbage in mind, just as Beaumont and Fletcher had written leading roles to showcase my talents. I regretted that Master Shakespeare had retired. I knew that I could play an outstanding romantic hero. But I still had Fletcher and Massinger to write for me. I looked forward to many future triumphs at the Globe.

The Globe was an outdoor theatre so I had to project my voice further if I wanted to be heard. The groundlings in the pit were an additional challenge. They could make or break a player. At the start of a performance, they would stand munching apples, cracking hazelnuts and swigging beer from bottles as they waited to be entertained. But if they grew restive, they would hurl them at the stage. They adored Master Burbage and would cheer his every appearance. However, I was a newcomer and fair game. Fortunately, I was soon able to win them over and within a short time I was their darling. Master Burbage took it all in good part.

"It is good to be popular, Nat. It builds your confidence as a player. But don't let it distract you from your craft. It takes a lifetime to gain the full mastery."

But in my arrogance, I set aside his counsel. I had youth, beauty and grace on my side. I could make my audience weep, laugh or watch in spellbound silence while I gave my speeches. I felt that I fully deserved my fame. Master Burbage was sparing with his praise, but seemed satisfied with my performances. One day, after the close of a play he called me over. "You should change your name, boy," he said seriously. "Field is the name of a peasant. You should pick something more effective that the crowds will remember."

"I will do my best to make it a field of honour," I retorted. I had no quarrel with my name. But I had kept my family background a secret from the rest of the company. I could only imagine their reaction if they knew that my father and my brother were both Puritan preachers. They strongly disapproved of players as vagabonds and sinners. My brother Theophilus had written an incendiary letter to me when he learned that I had joined the King's Men. He had done well for himself and was now a royal chaplain.

> *"It was one thing for you to be one of the queen's performers when you were a child. But now that you are a grown youth you should give careful consideration to your path in life. Our father would not have wanted this for you. These public plays are full of wanton gestures and bawdy speeches. They are the occasion of sin to both yourself and others. The life of a player is one of folly and vice. It is the broad and common way that leads to destruction. I urge you to leave it for the sake of your soul. If you come to me, I will employ you as my clerk until you can find a better use for your talents. I will keep you daily in my prayers in the hope that you will see the light and turn away from this vanity."*

I smiled inwardly as I read the familiar Puritan diatribe. Only a fool would give up their hard-won skills and settle for a life of drudgery as a clerk. My brother would never understand that the life of a player was ideally suited to my talents. I would never willingly leave it. The theatre was now the whole world to me. It was full of opportunities for a man of ambition to make his fame and fortune. I had made plans for my future. I would become a leading actor and a shareholder in the theatre. And I would continue my efforts at being a playwright. I hoped that one day I would be as famous as Master Shakespeare and Master Jonson. And so, I continued to write.

In February 1616, Master Jonson achieved his dearest wish. He was summoned to court to be honoured by the king and queen for his work as a poet and playwright. He was appointed as the first poet laureate of England and granted a royal pension of one hundred marks per year. He was radiant with joy.

"I cannot thank your Majesties enough for your generosity," he said. "I am deeply honoured and profoundly grateful."

"It is we who are grateful for your marvellous court masques, Master Jonson," replied the queen graciously. "They have made England the wonder of Europe!"

The courtiers swarmed over to congratulate him upon his success, pay him their compliments and ply him with glasses of wine. By the end of the evening, he could hardly stand. I decided that I had better take charge of him and accompanied him back home to his lodgings in Blackfriars.

"It was a triumph, Nat, a glorious triumph!" he declared. "Did you see how the whole court paid its homage to me? Finally, the world has recognised my true worth as a man of letters. How long have I waited! How much had I despaired of ever gaining any renown!"

"It was very well deserved, Master Jonson," I assured him. "The queen said the same thing herself."

"She is a most gracious lady and I believe that I have her to thank for this honour. King James is only generous to his fellow Scots and his young bedfellows. But now my fortunes are made. One day I shall be appointed as the Master of the Revels!"

We arrived at his home and I helped him to remove his boots. But he was loathe to have me leave. He wanted to retain his audience and relive the glorious moment when the royal court had gathered in his honour. It was late and I was weary, but I decided to humour him.

He sat down on his high-backed chair while I struggled to light a half-burned candle in the darkness. "It vindicates me, Nat, do you know that?" he said with satisfaction. "All my denigrators will grind their teeth into powder when they hear of my good fortune! You know how they sneered at me as a man of lowly birth and said that I should return to my former trade of bricklaying. They have always dismissed my scholarship, but now it has been honoured by the highest in the land! It makes up for all those years of struggle and hardship. There were times when I spent my last few pence on paper and ink when I had neither bread nor fuel in the house."

The following morning, Master Jonson was as sick as a dog. But it did not quench his spirits in the least. He still gloried in the memory of his accolades. "I must do something to memorialise this great occasion, Nat," he announced. "I am going to see my printer today. I shall commission a Folio edition of my collected plays and poems."

In due course, the Folio edition of his writing was published. "*The Workes of Benjamin Jonson,*" contained nine plays, two books of poetry, thirteen masques, and six entertainments. It was the first time that any English writer had published a collection of their writing and some of his rivals mocked his pretensions:

"Pray tell me, Ben, where doth the mystery lurk,
What others call a play you call a work?"

But Master Jonson took no notice of their spite. He commandeered the largest table in the Mermaid tavern and ordered a dozen bottles of their best canary wine. Then he gathered his friends together and took great delight in boasting of his achievements:

"I have not lived in vain, my friends! I have achieved something of note after all. Fleeting Fame and Fickle Fortune have at last condescended to crown my endeavours!"

We toasted Master Jonson on his success as the first poet laureate of England and took it in turns to read our dedicatory verses on his Folio. He was lauded as a second Horace, an outstanding writer and dramatist, and an accomplished translator. His close friend and fellow poet, Hugh Holland, led the tributes with a verse in praise of his many works:

"A Master, read in flatteries great skill,
Could not pass truth, though he would force his will,
By praising this too much, to get more praise
In his Art, than you out yours do raise.
Nor can full truth be utter'd of your worth,
Unless you your own praises do set forth:
None else can write so skilfully to show
Your praise: Ages shall pay, yet still must owe.
All I dare say, is, you have written well;
In what exceeding height, I dare not tell."

When all the other writers had read their epigrams, I concluded the commendations with a verse in honour of the plays in which I had performed so many times:

*"Each like an Indian Ship or Hull appears
That took a Voyage for some certain years
To plow the Sea and furrow up the Main,
And brought rich Ingot, from his loaden Brain.
His Art the Sun; his Labours were the Lines,
His solid stuff the Treasure of his Lines."*

"Bravo, young Nat! We will make a poet of you yet!" replied Master Jonson. "I thank all of the assembled company for their golden opinions which far exceed my poor deserts as a humble artist and captive of the Muse. And now I drink a toast to friendship! Let us be merry my friends!"

The night passed most pleasantly with many more epigrams, anecdotes and further toasts. Afterwards, I walked Master Jonson back home to his lodgings. He was in a vastly contented mood.

"I am greatly blessed in my friends, Nat," he declared. "No other writer has ever received such honourable tributes. It was most gratifying to hear!"

"It is a pity that Master Shakespeare was not there," I remarked. "I am sure that he would have written you a splendid accolade."

My passing comment sparked a reaction. "Indeed, it was a great shame that he could not be present tonight," he mused. "It was such a fine gathering of wits. I am certain that he would have enjoyed it immensely."

"Perhaps you could write a letter to him and tell him of your recent successes?" I proposed.

"Write to him? No indeed!" he declared. "We shall go to see my old friend Will in Stratford. He must miss his life in the metropolis."

I was astonished by this sudden announcement. "Stratford? But that's three days journey from London," I exclaimed.

"Why not?" he replied. "It is good to see something of the world outside London. I have my pension now so I can afford to make the trip. I'll bring him some copies of the latest printed plays. You should take the opportunity to make his acquaintance. I shall send him a letter to expect us."

I realised that Master Jonson craved the plaudits of his former rival more than any other man. We hired two horses from the carrier William Greenaway for ten shillings and rode them to Stratford. We stayed in country inns along the way. It reminded me of my trip to Hardwick Hall many years before. Master Shakespeare lived at New Place on Chapel Street. It was a three-storey building made of brick and timber. He knew Master Jonson very well and made us very welcome. He invited us to sit outside in his garden and take our ease before dinner. A great oak spread its shade above us. I could see that Master Jonson looked thoughtful. He had no house in the countryside for his retirement. He looked about him appraisingly.

"I confess that I have not acted with your wisdom and forethought, Will," he said ruefully. "Unfortunately, London is a place of temptations. It beguiles you into enjoying the pleasures of the day and you end up taking no thought for the morrow."

"Very true," he agreed. "Lady Metropolis is a seductive mistress. Once she has you in her toils it is hard to break free."

"Are you working on anything, Will?" he asked him.

Master Shakespeare shook his head. "I write sonnets for my own pleasure. I don't suppose anyone else will ever read them. But it is no matter for there is plenty to occupy me here. I have my garden to keep and my accounts to keep square. In my lodgings in London, I used to dream of my pleasant house in Stratford. I stayed away too long from here. I left my wife and children to make shift without me while I made a name for myself in the theatre. It was selfish of me. I realise that now."

"But then the world would never have heard of you, Will!"

He shrugged. "Fame is but a bauble. You know it as well as I do. I never wanted to be one of those strutting fools at court, fawning on the mighty and spurning those below them. Life is better here in the countryside. People live in better charity with each other than the placemen of the court. I have had my time in the sun and now I am content to sit in the shade and rest. And what of you, Ben? I hear good reports of your royal entertainments from my friends," he said.

"My detractors call them toys," he admitted. "They have not the weight nor substance of my plays. But they have been well received at court and I have been handsomely rewarded for my trouble by the queen. Indeed, I have recently been honoured by their Majesties with a pension of a hundred pounds a year." He darted a look at Master Shakespeare to see how he would take the news. But he was genuinely pleased for him.

"It is very well deserved, Ben," he said heartily. "You have done them good service with your pen and it is only right that they should acknowledge it."

Mistress Shakespeare was a good hostess and she provided a generous table for our dinner. It consisted of fine baked bread, tasty pottage and a shoulder of mutton.

"We do not get such fine vegetables in London," said Master Jonson.

"They are from our garden," she said proudly. "They were freshly picked today."

"It was a splendid mutton, Mistress Shakespeare" he continued. "And I congratulate you upon your delicious ale."

"My wife keeps a fine table," agreed Master Shakespeare. "But the best beer in Stratford is found at the Old Thatch tavern. It is so strong that it could knock out a prize bull. You must try it while you are here. You shall be my guests there tonight!"

"Not at all, countered Ben. You shall be my guest, Will."

"Then we shall take turns to toast each other! Agreed?"

Mistress Shakespeare was not pleased by this talk of taverns. "I don't know why you want to spend the evening in that dirty old place," she scolded. "Everyone knows that 'tis full of fleas. And it is a waste of coin besides. You would do better to drink here at home!"

"We won't be long my dear," he replied. "My friends must see something of the town."

"Don't stay out all night or you'll catch a chill in that drafty old barn," she snapped.

Mistress Shakespeare was not mistaken in her assessment of the Old Thatch tavern. I was not much taken by the crude furniture, the old rushes on the floor and the fleas. But Master Shakespeare was given a warm welcome by the other patrons. We sat down at a trestle table and called for a round of their best beer. Three large tankards were set down before us. Master Jonson proposed a toast. "To my dear friend and master, William Shakespeare!" Then he took a draught. "That is a drop of the right stuff, Will," he exclaimed. I tried it gingerly. It was certainly very potent.

The two old friends fell to reminiscing together about their early lives as players and writers with the Lord Admiral's Men and Lord Chamberlain's Men.

"Master Shakespeare did me a good service in my youth, Nat," said Master Jonson, easing himself back on his chair. "When I wrote *"Every Man in his Humour,"* I offered it to the Lord Chamberlain's Men. John Heminges gave it a cursory look and told me that it would be of no service to them. But Master Shakespeare happened to be present and took it into his hands for perusal. He found something in it that he liked and persuaded Heminges that the players should read it through before they made a decision. They agreed to stage it and it became my first success."

"I played the role of Kno'well in the play," remarked Master Shakespeare. "It was a fine comedy and deserved its success."

"You always did like to play the older characters, Will," remarked Master Jonson.

"Well, I was best suited to them. I was tall and gangly as a young man. Not like this young Adonis here who was made to play romantic leads."

"Yes, Nat was the darling of the stage even when he was only a boy-player," Master Jonson agreed. "You should have seen him play the lead in *"Cynthia's Revels."* Nobody had ever seen anything like it!"

"I am sorry that I missed it," he said courteously. "I have heard of you, young man. My colleague Dick Burbage speaks well of your talents on the stage."

"What advice do you have for my young friend?" asked Master Jonson.

He studied me for a moment with his dark, intelligent eyes. "Tell the truth, boy! Be a truthful performer!"

I longed to ask him if he had heard of my plays. But I did not dare to speak of them in the presence of two such great writers. The moment passed and I lost my opportunity to discuss the art of comedy with the best playwrights of the day. Afterwards, I regretted it and cursed myself for bring such a tongue-tied fool. I knew that I would never get such a chance again. More rounds of beer were consumed as Master Jonson regaled Master Shakespeare with the latest gossip from London. My head grew thick and the two friends became more and more incoherent in their toasts to each other. Finally, Master Shakespeare slumped over on the table.

Master Jonson shook his head. "Poor old Will! He never did have a good head for drink!" We carried him home between us and put him to bed. Mistress Shakespeare had a great deal to say when she saw the state of her husband.

"I knew how 'twould be going out carousing late at night! 'Tis better for a man of your dignity to remain quietly at home before his own fireplace and sup his own ale!" Master Jonson was fulsome in his apologies, but she remained implacable.

"You fine London gentlemen ought to be ashamed to bring him home in such a condition," she scolded. She fussed around making him a posset while Master Jonson and I prudently withdrew to our beds.

"She is as great a shrew as my wife," he observed. "No wonder Will spent all his time in London!"

The following morning, we thanked to Mistress Shakespeare for her hospitality and set off back to London. Not long after our return, we heard the sad news of Master Shakespeare's death from a fever. I wondered if too much Old Thatch beer had carried him off. His death was felt as a great loss to the theatre. Two of his colleagues, John Heminges and Henry Condell, decided to print a collection of thirty-six of his plays as a tribute to his memory. My name was included in the list of players who had performed his plays at the Globe theatre. Master Jonson wrote a dedicatory verse for the folio in praise of his immortal genius:

> *"Sweet Swan of Avon! What a sight it were*
> *To see thee in our waters yet appear,*
> *And make those flights upon the banks of Thames,*
> *That so did take Eliza and our James!"*

Now the great man would write no more. But the memory of our recent meeting inspired me to take up my pen anew and I began to write a new play. It was a comedy called *"Women Pleased."* I showed some pages from the first act to Master Burbage.

"Do you fancy yourself as the next Shakespeare, lad?" He shook his head. "You'll never be his equal."

"I don't aspire to be his equal," I retorted sharply.

He saw my downcast looks and relented. "Very few writers can match the poetry of his language. But you have a fine comic gift of your own, Nat. So, keep at it. The theatre always needs new material."

He swept off leaving me disconsolate. A fine comic gift indeed! I composed my own plots for my plays. I didn't take them out of dusty old histories. And I knew how to craft a play for the stage and how to match the parts to the talents of the players. Would I always be compared to others? But if I was honest with myself, I was bound to admit that I lacked the creative genius of my friends Fletcher and Beaumont. My plots were inferior to theirs. I set the work aside. It was better not to write at all than to be thought second-rate. I repaired to the Mermaid tavern to console myself with good wine and good company. There I met my good friend Master Fletcher. He hailed my arrival with delight and urged me to join with him in writing more plays. Francis Beaumont had sadly died of a fever and he needed a partner for his next work.

"I know that you've joined the King's Men and you're busy with your acting, but it's good to have other irons in the fire," he urged me. "I've got a new idea for a play and there's a young writer I know called Philip Massinger. We could make up a trio like we did with Beaumont."

I decided that collaboration was more profitable than labouring to produce my own dramas. It would be better to work with Master Fletcher and play to my strengths as a writer. I knew that I excelled in contriving witty dialogues and comic situations. The outcome would be mutually beneficial. Around this time a great scandal had erupted at the court. The king's favourite, Viscount Rochester, had risen to become the earl of Somerset and the Lord Chamberlain. He had married the former Lady Frances Howard after her divorce from the earl of Essex. Now he and his wife had been put on trial for the murder of a man named Thomas Overbury. It was the talk of all the taverns. The king had taken a new favourite called George Villiers. He was another handsome nonentity. I felt a moment of sympathy for the former favourite. Despite his vigilance, it seemed that someone else had replaced him after all. And having reached the pinnacle of success, he had lost everything for the love of a woman.

"What a splendid play we could make of it!" I said to my fellow writers. "It has all the elements of a successful drama. He is a perfect example of a man with a fatal flaw. He had everything he could want in life, but he lost it all through his lack of good judgement."

"If it were not for the Master of the Revels and the Privy Council," observed Master Massinger. He was a shy young man but he shared our sense of humour.

"We could call it *"The Rise and Fall of Lord Somerset,"*" I proposed. "It would be the greatest success in London!"

"It would be better to call it *"The Rise and Fall of Lord Nincompoop"* and make it a comic satire," he replied with a grin.

"It would have to be given another name entirely to have a chance. How about calling it *"The King's Favourite"* and set it in another country in the distant past," I suggested.

"Samuel Daniel tried that ruse with *"Philotas"* but he didn't get away with it," he remarked, shaking his head.

"We would all find ourselves in prison," said Master Fletcher firmly. "The king would never forgive us for dramatizing his friend's misfortunes. There are plenty of safer subjects to choose."

We decided that our first joint venture would be a tragicomedy called *"The Queen of Corinth."* It was set in ancient Greece so we did not anticipate having any trouble with the censors. We discussed the plot and then split the play up between us. When it was completed, we planned to sell it to the *King's Men*.

CHAPTER 13

The Toast of London

"If you will learne howe to bee false and deceyue your husbandes, or husbandes their wyues, howe to playe the harlottes, to obtayne one's love, howe to ravishe, howe to beguyle, howe to betraye, to flatter, lye, sweare, forsweare, how to allure to whoredome . . . shall not you learne, then, at such enterludes howe to practise them?"

(John Northbrooke, A Treatise wherein Vaine Playes are Reproved, 1577).

"Do they not maintain bawdry, insinuate foolery, and renew the remembrance of heathen idolatry? Do they not induce whoredom and uncleanness? Nay are they not rather plain devourers of maidenly virginity and chastity?"

(Philip Stubbes, The Anatomie of Abuses, 1583).

In the autumn of 1616 Master Jonson wrote a new play called *"The Devil is an Ass."* It was a comedy in which the devil took on human form and attempted to navigate the streets of London. Master Burbage played the devil and I played a foolish gentleman named Fabian Fitzdottrel. The first performance at the Globe was a tremendous success.

The audience called the players back onstage again and again to take their applause. Above the noise, I heard my name being called: "Nat! Nat!" Master John Heminges was delighted. The other players wanted to sweep me off to a tavern and stand me rounds of drinks to celebrate. But for once, I put them off and promised that I would join them later. I wanted to be alone for a while to take in this intoxicating sensation. I changed out of my fine costume and went to sit on the edge of the stage. The sun hung low in the sky, casting a warm glow over the dusty yard. The crowds had departed and only a few odd job men were left collecting up the rubbish left on the floor. But it seemed that I could still hear faint echoes of the applause. Then I spotted an orange girl lingering at the side of the yard. Suddenly I realised that I was parched with thirst. I approached her, my throat dry and cracked.

"Got any left?" I croaked, my voice barely audible. She turned to me, her gaze steady, and nodded. She wore an old patched gown with an apron and mismatched shoes. The orange sellers were among the poorest of the poor. But there was grace in her stance, a quiet defiance against the odds. I held out my hand to her expectantly. At once, her eyes narrowed, assessing me. She was no stranger to the art of negotiation.

"They're sixpence each," she replied.

"Only during the show," I countered.

She hesitated for a moment and then shook her head. "I can't go giving them away. I'd never hear the last of it from old mother Meggs."

"Didn't you see my performance today? I said with my most persuasive smile. "Don't you think I deserve one? A moment of sweetness to balance the toil."

"Deserve?" Her eyes lit up with mischief and her voice held a hint of amusement. "Deserve is a slippery word, my friend. You might – and then again you might not. How could a simple girl like me possibly know the truth?" I admired her adroit repartee. Surely, such a girl deserved better than to hawk her wares around a noisy, bustling theatre day after day. I leaned closer, catching the faint scent of citrus.

"I've performed for kings and queens," I boasted. "Today I've made an entire crowd weep and laugh. It's no wonder that I'm thirsty. Is an orange really too much to ask?"

"You are a rogue!" she replied with a ripple of laughter. "Go on then. I shall have to say that a thief stole one out of my basket." She tossed me an orange and I caught it deftly. It was sweet and juicy and I rapidly devoured it. I looked up to see that the girl was still there.

"It's good!" I said politely.

"Of course! They're the finest quality. You can't sell rotten ones in the theatre. Folks wouldn't ever buy from me again. I'm known for the best fruit and sweets in London!" She smiled and her face lit up with pleasure. She had long dark hair and blue eyes. At that moment she looked like a pretty maid out for a stroll in the city.

"What's your name, mistress?" I asked, touched by the pride she took in her humble occupation.

"It's Molly Meggs," she replied. "But everyone calls me Orange Moll." I nodded, watching as she adjusted the weight of her basket.

"What are you going to do now, Molly?" I queried. Now that the performance was over, I felt an overwhelming sense of emptiness. I wanted her to keep me company a little longer.

"I shall have to go out to sell the rest of them along the Bankside. I can't go home till my basket's empty."

"Stay here and talk to me, Molly," I urged her. "Leave your basket here. I'll keep it safe till tomorrow."

Molly's eyes flickered with uncertainty. "I can't return without it. I'll get beaten."

"Tell mother Meggs that a gang of boys ran off with it," I suggested.

"We don't have another basket," she demurred. She pulled it closer and stepped away. My heart sank with disappointment. Just then Master Heminges stepped out onto the stage.

"Still here, Nat?" he said in surprise. "I was just closing up. I thought you'd be out celebrating with the rest of the company."

"It's still early, Master Heminges," I replied. He had been checking the receipts in the box office. And he looked like a man who was well satisfied.

He thrust his hand into his sleeve and drew out a pouch. "Say nothing to the others, but take this as a token of my esteem. You have well deserved it!" He handed me a gold crown. I was astonished by this munificence. I wondered how much profit he had made that day.

"I am most grateful, Master Heminges," I exclaimed.

"I am generous to those who merit it," he remarked with satisfaction and left me to contemplate my unexpected good fortune. Molly gazed at me with envy. I was struck by a sudden thought.

"How many oranges have you got left, Molly?" I asked her.

"Four of them," she said with a sigh. It was the wrong time of day to try to sell oranges and no-one knew it better than her.

A sudden inspiration struck me and I smiled. "I'll buy your oranges, Molly."

"Oh, would you?" she said gratefully.

"And I'll pay you for the other one too. Take the crown and give me back two shillings."

Molly climbed onto the stage as nimbly as a goat and placed the basket of oranges in front of me. I handed her the gold crown and she counted out four sixpences. As our fingers touched, I felt a spark of fire surge through me.

"No need to hurry away, Molly," I said. "Sit down here next to me. We have the whole theatre to ourselves."

"What if we get locked in here?" she objected.

"The gatekeeper knows me," I assured her. "He'll let us out."

As the sun dipped lower in the sky, I leaned over and kissed her. "You are my best reward, Molly. You are fairer than a gillyflower and sweeter than an orange."

She touched my face tenderly. "You are as handsome as a prince. I wish that I was a fine lady and not an orange girl."

"On this stage poor young men can become noblemen and kings. So why shouldn't you become a duchess or a queen?" I asked. Molly listened to my words in delight.

"You talk as fair as a prince too. I could listen to you talk all day," she sighed and nestled closer. I was glad that I had not gone with the others to spend the evening in the fusty tavern.

"I will be a gallant knight and you will be my fair mistress," I declared, my heart pounding like a hundred hooves on a battlefield. The air was thick with anticipation, and the theatre walls seemed to lean in, listening to my whispered promises. "I love nothing in the world so well as you," I continued, my voice unwavering. Her eyes, like sapphires in the twilight, held mine captive. In her face, I saw not just a fair maiden, but a queen who would reign over my soul forevermore. I slid my arms around her waist and embraced her. She did not resist me. In that moment I felt that I would cross kingdoms and slay dragons to keep her by my side.

The moon was rising and the theatre was dark when we finally left. The gatekeeper was asleep and cursed me for rousing him. I had to part with a sixpence to persuade him to unlock the door. I gave Molly one last kiss before she fled into the night. From then on, we spent all our evenings together. My comrades jibed at me for shunning the tavern. When they discovered my relationship with Molly, they teased me mercilessly for preferring the company of such a common girl. I knew they despised her as a mere orange seller, but I didn't care what they thought. An actor had no cause to be vain and Molly was the sweetest girl in London. I vowed to be her protector, her champion, and her heart's truest desire. I recited lines from love scenes and imagined that she was Juliet and I was her Romeo. But our idyll was cut cruelly short. Master Heminges summoned me into the box office. A buxom woman dressed in a tattered cambric gown was standing there.

"Is he the one?" she demanded. "You leave my Molly be. She comes to the theatre to sell oranges not to dally with the likes of you. I doubt you've got two shillings to rub together."

I felt the blood rush to my head at her insulting words. The manager shook his head and gave me a disapproving look. "We haven't done any harm," I protested.

"So, you say! My Moll's got to earn her living. But her head's full of day-dreams because of you. She's brought home her basket half-full for the past fortnight. I'll have no more of such goings-on. You're not to go near her again!"

Master Heminges held up his hand. "I assure you, Mrs Meggs, that there will be no further association between them. You have my word as a gentleman." She flounced out of the door in triumph.

"We don't want any trouble, Nat," he warned me. "The orange girls are here for work not romance. You're not a young lord to take one as your mistress."

I was crushed by the end of our happy romance. From then on, Molly and I could only exchange looks from afar. Her lovely eyes were full of tears. The power of the stage had misled me. We were still just a poor boy and girl. We couldn't live on our love. I wished that I had the means to support us both, but it was an impossible dream. It would take me years to gain my independence. I still had my career to build and my fortune to make. I vowed that I would succeed and then I would be free to love as I chose.

In time, I got over my heartbreak for Molly. Her mother married her to a prosperous grocer and she no longer frequented the theatre. I paid no attention to any of the other orange girls. I knew now that romantic plays were mere fictions. But plenty of other women attended the theatre. And there were many who come to see the handsome young actors of the company. I was not short of admirers. They included young girls, handsome wives and rich widows. I received letters full of compliments and invitations to dine. Some of them were accompanied by expensive gifts. I knew that I was in no position to court a girl and that to dally with a respectable wife risked causing a scandal. But the widows were another matter. They could manage their own affairs and spend their income as they chose. If they wanted to make much of me, it was no-one's concern. I soon gained a reputation as a regular libertine. My comrades teased me and called me the Romeo of the Bankside.

"You're only jealous," I retorted. My admirers were so generous that I could afford to dress as finely as a lord both on and off the stage. Their coin flowed like wine, and I drank deeply from their flattery. In return I repaid them with the charming attentions they craved. Whenever I took my applause, I directed my smiles in their direction. *"Encore,"* they cried. And I, with a flourish, stepped forward to make another bow. The manager made no objection. The widows tipped him handsomely in return for the privilege of my company in the evenings. They were shrewd ladies who understood the world and taught me how to live well. Ah, the life of a libertine! It was a masquerade of venal pleasures. But behind the bravado, my heart hungered for more than fleeting liaisons. They were no more satisfying than drinking a syllabub. Deep down I still longed for a love that would transcend mere conquest.

Dick Burbage grew concerned about my reckless behaviour and scolded me for it. "Nat, you are wasting your time and substance in pursuing these trivial romances. They are distracting you from higher things. A young actor and playwright should dedicate himself to his craft if he wants to be taken seriously."

"I have been dedicating myself to my craft since I was thirteen years' old," I retorted. "Why shouldn't I combine business with pleasure?"

"No-one would object to a little pleasure, Nat. It is only natural. But you have set aside your writing to indulge yourself in folly. You still have your name and fortune to make."

"Consider it research into human nature, my friend. I cannot learn about life just by acting parts on the stage. I must explore the depths of love, passion and jealousy for myself. Otherwise, my writing will never be authentic."

"You have a ready answer for everything, Nat. But you are in danger of becoming a mere fribble and ne'er do well. Don't throw away your talents in pursuing these meaningless liaisons."

"Next you will be telling me to settle down and marry."

"You are becoming a poor imitation of Ralph Roister-Doister. It is a shame to see you lose your promise and take up these bad ways."

I made up the quarrel with Dick and promised to make amends. I dutifully attended the morning rehearsals and learned my parts so perfectly that he had no cause to disapprove of me. I became more circumspect about conducting my romances. I took my admirers' presents to the pawnshop and saved up the proceeds instead of wasting them at taverns and gambling dens. In short, I became the model of an aspiring young actor for I had a plan in my mind. Master Heminges was pleased with my conduct. I had become a draw for the audience of the Globe and a boon for the box-office. I asked him if he would be willing to do me a favour.

"I would be glad to do anything in my power, Nat. Just name it!" he said expansively.

"You are our business manager and the other players in the company look to you for guidance."

"I hope that they regard me as someone who is worthy of their trust," he replied complacently.

"I have saved up the sum of one hundred pounds. It would be a dream come true for me to become one of the shareholders of the theatre. Would you be willing to speak to the others on my behalf?"

"It is a high aspiration, Nat. You are only a young man and you have not been a member of our company for long. But your request has merit and I shall put it before the other shareholders at our next meeting."

I was sure that Dick would support me and that Master Heminges would persuade the rest. After all, I was a popular actor and they would not want to lose me to a rival company. And so, it turned out. I was invited to become one of the shareholders of the theatre. From now on, I would attend their meetings and I would enjoy a share of the profits from every performance. I made a graceful speech of thanks to the company:

"Gentlemen, I thank you for your patronage and support. It has been an honour to perform as a player in such a prestigious company. But it is an even greater distinction to be accepted as one of your illustrious shareholders. I will make it my constant endeavour to be worthy of your trust and regard."

Master Burbage rolled his eyes and pursed his lips at my bombast. But Master Heminges thanked me in return and foretold that I would have a brilliant future at the Globe. He announced that our next play would be "*The Mad Lover*" by Beaumont and Fletcher and I would play the part of Astorax, the king of Paphos. I revelled in his compliments and my success. Everything was falling into place for me.

On 5th January 1617 the King's Men presented "*The Mad Lover*" at court as part of the Christmas festivities. Master Burbage was outstanding in the role of General Memnon, the mad lover of the title, and the play was very well received. The following day it was Twelfth Night and I appeared as Mercury in the "*Masque of Pleasure Reconciled to Virtue.*" Prince Charles Stuart also appeared in the masque in the role of a virtuous prince. The anti-masque featured a dozen men dressed in barrels, and a dozen boys costumed as frogs. A second anti-masque featured a dance of pygmies. The main masque took the theme of Hercules at the crossroads. He had to choose between two ways. Finally, he rejected Vice and chose the path of Virtue. The masque began dramatically with a scene of Hercules holding up Mount Atlas. The mountain's peak was shaped like a human head that moved its eyes and changed expression. But the masque failed to live up to its early promise. The rest of the scenery was dull and the speeches were flat.

The masque did not find favour with the king. Towards the end, he grew weary of listening to the long speeches and called for the dancers to return to the stage. The masquers danced the Spanish dance once more with their ladies. But because they were tired, their steps began to lag and they fell out of time. The king grew impatient and shouted loudly, "Why don't they dance? What did you make me come here for? Devil take all of you, dance!"

At that moment, George Villiers, the duke of Buckingham stepped into the breach. He sprang forward and danced a number of high capers with such grace and lightness that he amazed everyone. His impromptu performance managed to calm the rage of the angry king, but it caused whispers to spread throughout the court about his lack of gentility. The masque proceeded to the end, although the king was still pouting as I gave the final speech in praise of virtue:

"She it is, in darkness shines,
Tis she that still hir-self refines
By hir owne light, to everie eye,
More seene, more knowne, when vice stands by.
And though a stranger here on earth
In heaven she hath hir right of birth.
There, there is Virtues seat
 Strive to keepe her your owne,

*'Tis only she, can make you great
Though place here, make you knowne."*

Afterwards, Master Jonson quarrelled with Master Inigo Jones over the failure of the masque. "It was your scenery that was to blame!" he stormed. "They showed neither novelty nor invention. Where were your devices?"

"Not, so!" he retorted. "It was your interminable speeches that provoked the king! Your poetry has grown so dull that you should return to your old trade of bricklaying again!"

Master Jonson was enraged. He vowed that he would never collaborate with him again. He turned his attention to staging his new plays at the Globe theatre. That year, I performed in *"Volpone"* and *"The Alchemist"* which were both great successes. Master Burbage played the leading roles and I played the second leads. I also appeared in *"The Queen of Corinth"* which I had written with Fletcher and Massinger. The virtuous Queen of Corinth planned a marriage between the ruler of Argos and her young ward Merione. But her villainous son Theanor was furious at being deprived of his intended bride and plotted to take his revenge. The play was another success and we congratulated each other on our partnership. It seemed that the public could not get enough of us. We agreed to meet again soon and plan our next drama.

CHAPTER 14

The Star-Crossed Lovers

*"For thy sweet love remembered such wealth brings
That then I scorn to change my state with kings"*

(Sonnet 29 by William Shakespeare)

In 1618 Fletcher, Massinger and I wrote *"The Knight of Malta"* and sold it to the King's Men for six pounds. Master Burbage played the villain Mountferrat, I played the heroic young knight Miranda and Jack Underwood played the role of my comrade Gomera. On the opening night of the performance, I stood in the wings in my costume. I looked out at the expectant crowds and smiled. I felt my powers stir within me. I knew that I would rule the stage this night! I was not mistaken in my expectations. I played the noble young hero Miranda to great acclaim. Afterwards, I sat in the players' room feeling spent but elated. The performance had been a complete triumph! There I received a message that a distinguished visitor wished me to come and give them a private reading. It was not uncommon for wealthy patrons to invite the leading players to act for them in their chambers.

"Another beguiled playgoer, eh Nat?" said Jack enviously. "If they saw you in your drunken state at the Mermaid, they would soon revise their opinion of you."

Every player hoped to attract a noble patron. They could buy you fine clothes, provide you with an income or give you a place in their household. At the least, I could expect to receive a purse of gold marks or a costly ring as a sign of favour. However, a different scenario awaited me. I made my way to Drury Lane as directed. It was an elegant townhouse such as the nobility built for their visits to London. A page was waiting for me by the entrance.

"Please come inside, Master Field," he said.

"Who is my host?" I enquired.

He raised his eyebrows at what he considered a foolish question. "My Lady Argyll."

I followed him into the reception chamber. The lady was sitting on a pink silk couch next to a roaring fire. She had finely arranged golden hair and wore a gown of blue satin with a parure of sapphires. She was clearly a very great lady indeed.

I took off my hat and made my best courtly bow. "I am honoured by your invitation, Lady Argyll."

She beckoned to me. "Come closer, so I may see you." I came and stood before the light of the glowing fire. I was still dressed in my nobleman's costume in which I cut a fine figure. I wore mouse-coloured velvet hose, a white taffeta doublet and a purple cloak.

"You are even more handsome in person than you are upon the stage," she said with open admiration. "What is your name, young man?"

"Master Nathan Field, at your service my lady," I replied.

"Your performance was quite heartbreaking, Master Field. I felt compelled to tell you so in person. You are the finest actor that I ever saw!"

"Thank you, my lady," I replied modestly. "I shall treasure your kind words."

"Such passion combined with such nobility of heart," she declared. "You are a man who could conquer any lady's heart!"

"I am glad that my performance pleased you, my lady," I replied. I was certain that she would press a splendid gift upon me and I could look forward to spending a merry night at the tavern. She reached out and touched my arm. I recognised that Lady Argyll had a romantic nature. She was picturing herself as Oriana and myself as Miranda. It was not an uncommon scenario. Unhappy wives and lonely widows were only too ready to fall into the arms of the dashing gallants of the stage after hearing them make their protestations of love. But Lady Argyll was no common playgoer. I would have to extricate myself carefully.

"My lady, you give me far too much credit," I said gently. "I am not the noble Miranda. I am only a humble actor. And I am not in the least noble. I am a poor man who is far beneath your notice."

"So modest!" she murmured. "But you need not fear to consort with me, Master Field. I am a wealthy woman and it is in my power to make you the happiest of men. I can raise you up and grant you anything that you desire. So do not fear to love me. Kiss me like you kissed the fair Oriana on the stage just now!" She gazed at me adoringly with wide blue eyes.

I was only human and Lady Argyll was young and fair. No man could possibly have resisted her. I gave her the kisses for which she longed and she gave me a heavy gold thumb ring set with a ruby.

"It is my own to give you, dear Nathan, for it belonged to my father," she insisted. I accepted it with humble gratitude. I knew that it would fetch a fine sum at the local pawnbrokers.

"I am deeply honoured, my lady," I replied.

"How I wish that I could become your patron, Master Field," she sighed. "But my husband does not care for the theatre. I fear that he would not allow it."

"Your true regard is the only reward I seek, my lady," I replied promptly.

"Indeed, you are a true artist, Master Field, devoted only to your craft. Unless you have a wife, of course."

"No, Lady Argyll. I do not have that happiness." I saw that she looked relieved. She wanted to see me as the ardent lover Miranda in truth as well as performance.

"When does your company perform again, Master Field?" she asked.

"Tomorrow, my lady," I replied.

"Then you shall meet me here again tomorrow and recite some more pretty speeches for me."

"As your ladyship wishes," I agreed. I could not help but observe the imperiousness with which she made her request. Indeed, it was more like an order. She was certainly familiar with the role of a great lady.

"Until tomorrow, Master Field," she whispered.

I returned home with my head spinning. This was unlike any assignation I had ever had before. Her passion for the theatre could make me rich. But somewhere beneath my excitement a note of warning sounded. I sensed that danger lay ahead. This was too good to be true! However, I dismissed it. This was the beginning of a piece of good fortune for me if I played my part as the lady desired.

At my next performance, I could not help but be conscious of her presence in the front row of the gallery. She hung upon my every word and applauded all my scenes. I found myself playing to her and rewarding her attention with tender looks and smiles. She smiled back in return. It was all part of the magic of the theatre. Still dressed in my costume, I retraced my steps to Drury Lane to meet my admirer. I was not in the least disappointed. She was even more entranced by my performance.

"Master Field, I have been a playgoer since my early youth," she confided to me. "But never before has a performance so ravished my heart as your portrayal of the noble Miranda. You are the perfect gentle knight of chivalry!"

"I am gratified to have made so happy an impression upon your ladyship," I replied with a bow.

"I must hear those lines again, Master Field!" she insisted.

"Certainly, my lady. Which lines would it please you to hear?" I asked with a beguiling smile.

"I pray you make your speech in praise of your beloved's eyes."

I took my stance before the fireplace so that I should be well illuminated. Then I turned towards Lady Argyll as if she were the virtuous Oriana: *"Thy pleas'd eyes send forth beams brighter that the star that ushers day."*

To my surprise she promptly replied in the words of Oriana defending her virtue: *"Miranda's deeds have been as white as Oriana's face, from the beginning to this point of time. And shall we now begin to stain both thus?"*

"How well your ladyship has remembered the part," I exclaimed.

"These words pierced my heart and burned themselves like flames upon my memory," she declared. "I can never forget them. I shall always treasure the true love between the noble lovers Miranda and Oriana! But the play is unfinished," she murmured invitingly.

"What do you mean, my lady?" I asked.

"For this space of time, I am Oriana and you are Miranda," she prompted.

I took my cue. "Dearest Oriana. What else is lacking in our meeting?" I enquired, my voice a soft murmur in the dimly lit chamber. The air was thick with anticipation, charged with the fire of forbidden desire.

"After the curtain falls, what happens next?" she whispered in my ear. Her voice sent shivers down my spine. Her words hung in the air, full of promise.

There could only be one answer. I set aside my prudence and my doubts. I pulled her close and took her in my arms. Our lips met and the world outside ceased to exist. In that moment we were the heroes of our own drama, bound by passion and fate. The curtain had fallen, but our story had just begun.

Our affair did not end there. Indeed, it was only the beginning. The following week, Lady Argyll sent for me again. She had fallen in love with me dressed as a nobleman on the stage. How could I disillusion her? I knew that I must dress in a manner that was worthy of such a great lady. I reclaimed her ring from the pawnbroker and wore it prominently on my finger. I purchased a new set of clothes regardless of the expense. Then I arrayed myself like a prince in my silk stockings, fair white linen, my splendid doublet and hose of yellow satin trimmed with gold lace and my feathered cap. My friends did not approve of such wanton extravagance.

Jack whistled at the sight of me. "Have you come into a fortune, Nat? You look like the Antichrist in that lewd hat!"

Dick Burbage scowled. "How much did you spend on those gauds?" he asked. "It is a folly!" It was true. My costume had cost me almost a year's wages. But I knew it would be worth it just to see the look of admiration in her eyes. He snorted when he saw the glowing ruby on my hand. I quickly turned the bezel around, but it was too late. "I don't suppose I need to ask you where you got that little trinket?" he remarked scathingly.

"All I can say is that it is a token from a very dear friend," I replied with dignity.

"You don't know your place, Nat," he scolded. "You're an actor, not a member of the gentry. You draw too much attention to yourself. No good will come of it."

"Life is different in London," I insisted. "A man can make his own way in the world and climb as high as he has a mind to do."

"You dress yourself too finely for a common man," he warned me. "You are not one of the princes that you play on the stage. And you cannot live as freely as a nobleman. Look at Edward Alleyn and William Shakespeare. They were both popular and successful and made their fortunes from the stage. They married, they bought their own houses and now they have retired to live in comfort. That is what any man of sense ought to do."

Is that all? I thought. *At least Master Jonson aspired to gain a post at court and win some acclaim for himself. He had urged me to find a wealthy patron and live under his protection. But I wanted to make my own way in the world.*

"I am not a common man," I retorted. "I have left my beginnings behind me. I intend to make my reputation on the stage and be remembered as a great actor and a great man."

"It is good for a man to have ambition. But it is dangerous to have too much. The nobility doesn't like commoners to rise too high in the world, no matter how much talent they have. Have you learned nothing from the tragic heroes you play on the stage?"

"They are just characters out of fictions. I have written them myself."

"Remember the fates of Wolsey, More and Cromwell. They were all common men who climbed too high. Their talent did not save them in the end."

I shrugged. "I don't serve in the court. Actors are seen as entertainers. They are not considered a threat by the powerful."

"That is where you are wrong. The theatre is kept under close scrutiny in case it fosters sedition or heresy. And too much popularity on the stage is seen as suspicious. Actors can easily be imprisoned on trumped up charges, assassinated by hired thugs or just disappear in the night. Look at what happened to Christopher Marlowe," he warned me.

"What did happen to Marlowe?" I enquired with interest.

"Nobody knows for sure. It was said that he died in a tavern brawl. But others said that he was one of the late queen's spies. He made himself enemies, but he laughed off the danger. He was a successful playwright and it made him too sure of himself. It is always wise for an actor to have a powerful patron to protect you from the envy and scorn of others."

"I am no brawler or spy. I am merely a popular actor. Why should the authorities bother with me?" I asked.

"You are the favourite of the playgoers right now. But remember that the favour of the crowds is fickle. It counts for nothing against the power of a vengeful nobleman. So never lampoon a public figure in any of your performances. You know, even Shakespeare had to apologise once for naming one of his characters after a Puritan nobleman."

"Who was that?" I asked him.

"Sir John Hardcastle in his play "*Henry IV*." He renamed him Falstaff."

I laughed, but he was in no mood to jest. "One day you will end up having a hole drilled in your ear," he scolded. "I fear that is what it will take to make you see sense. A Roman general was granted a triumph in Rome as his reward for gaining victory in battle. But in their wisdom, the senate placed a slave in the chariot to whisper in his ear, "*Remember, thou art mortal*!" They understood that hubris was the fatal flaw that undid many heroes."

"It is the theme of all historical tragedies, I replied impatiently. "What are you trying to say?"

"Not to fly too close to the sun, young Icarus."

I flinched as his words reminded me of the scornful words of Master Giles. But I was no longer a boy. I was a successful actor and a playwright. I had a share in the most prosperous theatre in London. I had more than achieved my ambitions. And I still had years ahead of me to accomplish even more. One day, I would be like Master Jonson and produce masques for the court. I had every confidence in myself.

Later that day, I presented myself at Drury Lane dressed in my splendid new doublet and hose. But I saw that her servants eyed me askance. They weren't deceived by my fine appearance.

"Can your servants be trusted not to gossip, Lady Argyll?" I asked her.

"I am not afraid of them," she pouted. "My husband amuses himself as he pleases. He has left me here to entertain myself as best I can. So, he has no reason to complain!"

I felt a pang of disquiet. A vengeful husband was a complication I could do without. A powerful nobleman could cause a great deal of trouble for a lowborn actor like me.

"You need not fear, my dear," she assured me. My husband never comes to the theatre. He has a great dislike for plays and thinks they are the greatest cause of immorality in society. Such folly! Whenever we come to London, he spends all his time at court attending the king. They go out hunting in the royal parks all day and I am obliged to find my own amusement at the playhouse. He has his own apartments at the palace and I am left quite alone in our townhouse. It is a sad state of affairs for a husband and wife."

I was relieved to know that our trysts would not be interrupted by his arrival. I smiled gallantly and kissed her hand.

"My dear, don't let's waste our time talking about him," she said ardently. "I bought this gown especially for you. Do you like it?"

I gave her the compliments she expected. "You are the fairest lady in the kingdom. I am not worthy of you, my love."

"Do not say so! I will not hear it. Your hands and your face are as pale and fine as any gentleman's. Your love-locks are as handsome as any gallant at the court. And you dress just as splendidly as a great nobleman. How could I not love you, dearest Nat?"

It was music to my ears. If she thought that we were well-matched then it was hard for me to disagree. We were both young, fair and passionate. We wanted to have lives full of beauty and romance. If she shared her luxuries with me and I shared my art with her, then surely it was a fair exchange? But I was living in a fool's paradise. If she was willing to forget the disparity in our stations, then the rest of world was certainly not. I should have taken warning from the expressions on her servant's faces. They were not prepared to tolerate such an aberration in their mistress. In their eyes, it was a greater presumption than Robert Dudley's courtship of Queen Elizabeth I. To my disappointment, my friend Jack shared their opinion. He was anxious and tried to warn me.

"It was bad enough when you were dallying with orange-sellers and bored housewives, Nat. But it is sheer folly to consort with a nobleman's wife. You will end up being run through with a rapier!"

But I was deaf to his entreaties. "Since when did you turn Puritan, Jack?" I retorted.

"You cannot pay court to a great lady without consequences," he said. "Particularly not a married lady. Adultery is a crime. You could be imprisoned. It's not worth it, Nat! Give it up, before it is too late!" I shrugged. I knew my fellow actors were jealous of my popularity. This was the ultimate proof of it. There was no way that Lord Argyll would want to risk publishing his shame to the world. If he found out, he would do everything possible to cover it up. There was nothing to fear. I realised that my dreams of gaining lasting fame and success on the stage paled into insignificance beside my surpassing love for Lady Argyll. I knew that I could not bear to live without her. She had become essential to my happiness.

"All my life I have been told what to do by others. But now I have finally found freedom and I intend to make the most of it."

"Don't you realise that Lord Argyll could send his men after you to avenge his honour? Why take such a foolish risk?"

"He can't do that! I am the darling of the London crowds. They would rally to my defence if anyone tried to attack me."

"You're not always on the stage, Nat. You're putting yourself in grave danger."

"True love pays no heed to danger. Her regard is all the reward I need. Besides, she has said that we can go away together if we are found out."

"And where do you think you could go? Really Nat, you are such a fool!"

But I thought it was the husband who was a fool to neglect so young and lovely a wife. Her admiration rapidly turned into infatuation. She attended every performance I gave and applauded every scene enthusiastically. We started meeting three times a week. Over time she told me of her life.

"My parents raised me to make an advantageous marriage," she sighed. "I was brought up to be the perfect wife for my future husband. And I married Lord Argyll who was a wealthy nobleman. It should have made me very happy. But he was a complete clod of a man. All that mattered to him was hunting and horses. He cared nothing for the finer things in life. He was bored by music, books and intelligent conversation. We had nothing to say to each other. He likes the country and I like the city. I should have married a man like you, Nat. How happy we would have been together!"

Once I would have been reminded of the comic play *"The Country Wife"* about a country-loving husband and his city-loving wife. But not now. Instead, I was deeply moved and wished that our stations in life were different so that we could have wed. As a testament to my love for her, I wrote her a poem and sent it to her. I entitled it: *"His Mistress, Lady May."*

"It is the fair and merry month of May,
That clothes the Field in all his rich array,
Adorning him with colours better dyed
Than any king can wear, or any bride.
But May is almost spent, the Field grows dun
With too much gazing on that May's hot sun,
And if mild Zephyrus, with gentle mind,
Vouchsafe not his calm breath, and the clouds kind
Distil their honey-drops, his heat to 'lay,
Poor Field will burn e'en in the midst of May."

Lady Argyll was delighted by my tribute. She arranged for me to have my portrait painted in the guise of the noble young hero Miranda. I wore a set of hose made of carnation silk and a doublet of cream silk. It was embroidered with flowers and butterflies and trimmed with gold lace around the collar and cuffs.

"I shall hang it in my boudoir and gaze upon it always," she sighed. "It will serve as a consolation to me whenever you cannot be here with me."

We were confident that our love would endure for the rest of our lives, unyielding to the winds of change or the tides of doubt. I had no wish to pursue any further dalliances. I knew that I had found the love of my life. Her laughter echoed through my mind and her touch ignited my deepest passions. In her eyes I saw the promise of a happy future and the fulfilment of my destiny.

My friend Dick invited me to come to dinner at his home. I thought it would be a pleasant social occasion. But it turned out that he wanted to speak to me seriously about my future as an actor.

"You are putting yourself in grave jeopardy if you continue down this path," he warned me. "I say this to you as a friend, Nat."

I was vexed and set down my goblet of claret on the table.

"I'm not the only one who has noticed. The other shareholders are concerned about you too."

"What is this – a meeting of the Star Chamber?" I snapped.

"Don't be flippant, Nat. I have only your best interests at heart. Break it off with this lady. If you continue your liaison, then you are risking a terrible scandal. And not just for yourself but for the whole theatre. There could be repercussions for all of us. We are only common players and we can't afford to make an enemy of someone like Lord Argyll. He has the ear of the king himself. If he decides to withdraw his patronage, we can no longer call ourselves the King's Men."

I realised that I would have to placate Dick. I did not want the entire company to turn on me. I understood that they must have delegated him to speak to me.

"Yes, you are quite right Dick," I said in my most reasonable voice. "Forgive me. I was not thinking of the risk to the theatre."

"Then you'll end your relationship right away?" he insisted.

"Yes, of course," I promised. "Only I must do it in the gentlest manner. She has a tender nature and I would not want to overthrow her health with a sudden renunciation."

He was satisfied and said no more on the subject. But I had no intention of breaking off my relationship with Lady Argyll. We had fallen so deeply in love that life without each other was unthinkable. I indulged in foolish fantasies that the inconvenient Lord Argyll might sudden die of a fall from his horse, or in a duel or from the plague. His wife would be left a rich widow and then we could marry. It did not occur to me that a widowed lady with a great fortune and property would never be allowed to throw herself away on a poor player. Her family would insist upon finding her a suitable match. We were destined to heartbreak regardless of whether he lived or died. Our mismatched love was the stuff of tragedy. But I was determined to protect our romance. I resolved that our future meetings would be entirely secret and the company would know nothing of them. I would tell Lady Argyll that we must take the utmost precautions. What a fool I was!

CHAPTER 15

Fallen from Heaven

"Fortune hath taken thee away, my love,
My life's soul and my soul's heaven above;
Fortune hath taken thee away, my princess;
My only light and my true fancy's mistress.
Fortune hath taken all away from me,
Fortune hath taken all by taking thee.
Dead to all joy, I only live to woe,
So, fortune now becomes my mortal foe"

(Fortune Hath Taken Thee Away, My Love by Sir Walter Raleigh)

Soon my affair with Lady Argyll had become an open scandal. But I was so carried away that I recklessly ignored the dangers. I hoped that Lord Argyll would stay in blissful ignorance on his country estate. Perhaps he would suffer a fatal accident while out hunting one day and then there would be no obstacle to our relationship. After all, stranger things had happened. But it was folly for me to imagine that our affair would remain a secret for long. I waited impatiently for my lady of Argyll to come to see me again. But she did not come. Days passed into weeks. I wondered if she was testing my love for her to see if I would stay true. At last, in August 1618, I received a message from her page boy.

"Have you read this letter, boy?" I asked him sternly.

"Oh, no, Master Field," he declared. I gave him a sixpence and told him to keep his mouth shut.

"You were never here, boy, do you understand? Now, be off with you!"

I shut the door and untied the ribband around the thin cylinder. I pressed the paper out flat and read the words. They were scribbled as if written in great haste, but they were unmistakeably in her hand.

"My love, the worst has happened. I am with child. I must at all costs keep it from Argyll. He will never forgive me for tarnishing his family name. I have gone to Spa in Belgium and given out that it is for my health. I must stay here until the child is born and I pray that there will be no scandal. Your unfortunate Anne."

Suddenly, my paradise came crashing down about my ears. It was a torment to be separated from my beloved Anne. I could not sleep for thinking about her. I longed to take a ship and go to be with her in Spa. But that would surely betray her secret. I would have to wait until the child was born. Then she could return to London and I could see her again. But three months later I received another message that dashed my hopes forever.

"My dear, we are discovered. My husband is taking me away to Brussels because of the scandal. He swears that he will never again permit me to visit the theatre. We cannot see each other again. Farewell for ever, my beloved Nat."

I crushed the paper between my fingers as the sharp pain of anguish pierced through me. Never to see each other again! I could hardly believe my misfortune. And a child! There would be a fine scandal if it were known that it was born out of wedlock. But Anne was a clever woman. She would contrive to cover the matter up. I tried to put the affair out of my mind. But the loss of my love affected me like a sickness. I had only her ring to remember her by. The image of her lovely face filled my mind by day and night. For the first time, my powers began to fail me. I lost my memory on the stage and I was forced to improvise in the midst of my speeches. The crowds were slow to notice my loss of concentration. But the other players noticed it at once.

"What on earth is wrong with you Nat?" said Jack. "You should lay off the sack before performances!"

Slowly, my nerve recovered and I regained my usual confidence. I accepted the loss of my lover. And I vowed that I would always treasure her memory in my heart. But then disaster struck! Someone in England had found us out. The rumour began to circulate around London. It became the latest society scandal.

"Lady Argyll is with child by Nat Field – a common actor on the stage!"

I wondered who had betrayed us. Was it that wretched page boy seeking a reward from his master? One of the household servants? Or had Anne foolishly confided in one of her friends? Whatever the case, the scandal was out there. I was prepared to deal with catcalls from the groundlings. I could give as good as I got from any heckler. I would just have to ride out the storm of censure until the next society scandal came along. But the worst was still to come. Master Heminges summoned me to a meeting of the shareholders. One look at their grim set of faces told me that I was done for.

"It's no good, Nat," he said with a frown. "We have to part company."

"What do you mean?" I exclaimed.

"News of your recent affair has reached the court. The king was most displeased to hear of it. And Lord Pembroke, the Lord Chamberlain, has ordered your dismissal from the company. There is nothing I can do."

I tried to reason with them. "It's just a stupid rumour. No-one can prove a thing."

"Unfortunately, your reputation as a ladies' man gives credence to it. And the earl of Argyll has a long arm. He is demanding your dismissal or else he threatens to close down the company as a danger to public morality."

"Suppose I retired to the country for a season until all this unpleasantness dies down?" I pleaded.

"You can never return to the theatre, Nat. This scandal has made too many waves at court. We are "*The King's Men*" and our reputation reflects upon him. The Lord Chamberlain himself has ordered your removal."

"So, you are dismissing me from the company."

"It would be better all round if you resigned voluntarily. We are prepared to buy out your share in the theatre."

And so, my life as a leading actor and playwright was ended with a snap of Argyll's fingers. It was like a scene out of one of my own farces where the cuckolded husband wreaks a final deadly revenge upon his rival. I had no idea where to go or what to do. To my astonishment, my brother Theophilus came to see me. He was now a great figure in the church for he had been appointed as the Bishop of Llandaff. I stared at him in disbelief. Had he come here to lecture me on my wicked ways, I wondered?

"You've heard, I take it," I said flatly.

"Yes, I've heard, Nat," he said compassionately. "It is the natural outcome of such a life as yours. But you are still a young man. There is time for you to turn to other endeavours. My offer to employ you as a clerk still stands. You can leave this sordid place and come to live in my household in Wales. You will find there are other worlds besides the theatre."

I shook my head. "It would only do you harm to take me in, Theophilus. I am the most notorious man in London and you are the Bishop of Llandaff. You can't possibly employ a former actor in your household."

He drew himself up and frowned slightly. At that moment he looked every inch the commanding figure of authority. It struck me what a splendid actor he would have made if he had not entered the church. "You are my brother, Nat," he declared. "No doubt I shall be criticised for taking you into my household. But it is safer for you to live here in Wales than in London. The duke of Argyll may send some of his men to settle the score with you. If anyone dares to object, I shall remind them of the blessed words of our Lord: *Judge not, lest ye be judged!*""

And so it was that I left London and travelled in a bishop's carriage to join the household of my brother in Llandaff. There I became the assistant to his secretary. I submitted to attend the daily services in his chapel and spent my days copying out his sermons in my best script. No doubt, Theophilus thought that such a worthy occupation would regenerate my soul. But inwardly, my heart was broken. I lived like banished Cain in my brother's household. Every day I ate the bread of charity. His servants despised me and his guests avoided me as a scandalous creature. I had no company apart from Theophilus and he had a thousand duties to occupy him. In the evenings I withdrew to my chamber to console myself with my library of books and playscripts. It was all that remained of my former life. But it was a bittersweet pleasure to peruse them now.

The loss of Anne was an endless source of pain and regret. I wondered if she pined for me or if she had forgotten me. Was she banished from society and from the theatre just like me? Did she have our child to comfort her or had her husband sent it away to punish her? I would never know and it grieved me. Our romance had been like a beautiful dream. But had our brief happiness been worth the terrible price that we had paid? I could not say. Now we were separated and outcast from what we loved the best. She was banished from the court and I was exiled from the theatre. Jack had been right. There was nowhere for our love to live and flourish in peace. All that was left was my bitter daily regret.

Dick Burbage was dead now. I wept when I heard the news. Who would replace him? He had brought to life all the heroes of Shakespeare just as splendidly as Edward Alleyn had portrayed the leading figures of Marlowe. I remembered how he had urged me to make my fortune and take a wife. But that noble aspiration was dead. There was no other woman in the world to compare with Anne. I gazed at her ring with its great blood-red ruby and sighed. Perhaps it would have been better if I had left it at the pawnshop and never returned to Drury Lane. She would have remained an honourable wife and countess and I would have remained the foremost actor in London. At night I dreamed that I was back treading the boards at the Globe in front of a cheering crowd or back at the tavern swapping stories with my friends. When I awoke, I cried with misery. I knew that I could never return to London. I would be too ashamed to face my old friends at the Mermaid. A life in exile was my only option.

But the loss of the theatre was an ongoing torment. I had fallen at the very height of my success and it was a bitter remembrance to me. There was not a day that I did not long to be back on the stage, making my bow at the curtain call and hearing the crowd roar out their appreciation. I could not believe that those days were gone forever. I fantasised that the groundlings would demand my return and the shareholders would write to me and invite me to return. But the London crowds were notoriously fickle. There were plenty of promising younger men rising through the ranks of the company who would eagerly take my place in their affections. I realised that I would never enthral the crowds again and I regretted my folly in becoming involved with a member of the nobility. I should have known that it would never end well. Why hadn't I contented myself by dallying with my numerous fair admirers of common birth? No-one would have cared if one of them had borne a by-blow to an actor.

I had fallen just as surely as Icarus in his foolish pride. I wept to think that never again would I dazzle an audience by my talent. I had years of performances still left in me but I knew that could never again set foot on the public stage. Nor could I write any more plays. I had become far too notorious for any company to associate themselves with me. it was all such a terrible waste! Nevertheless, during my days of weary copying, I found myself writing the scenes of a play in three acts. It would be my last work. It would tell the story of a young child who began as a boy-player, rose to conquer the London stage and then fell at the very peak of his talent. It would be a tragedy of our times. I would call it: *The Queen's Vagabond!*

EPILOGUE

Nathan Field died in 1620 at the age of 33 following a scandal that forced him to retire from the stage.

He is one of the few examples of an Elizabethan boy actor who became a leading player and a playwright as an adult.

He was the author or co-author of seven plays which were only moderately successful at the time and were forgotten after his death: *A Woman is a Weathercock and Amends for Ladies; The Honest Man's Fortune (1613), Four Plays in One (1613), The Queen of Corinth (1617), The Knight of Malta (1618), and The Fatal Dowry (1619).*

His main claim to fame was to be listed among the players of The King's Men in Shakespeare's First Folio which was published in 1623.

He was one of the last generations of boy actors who played female roles.

In 1661 women were finally allowed to perform on the public stage in England.

BOOK GROUP DISCUSSION GUIDE FOR "THE QUEEN'S VAGABOND"

---

(1) What did you think of the book's title? How does it relate to the book's contents? What other title might you choose?

(2) What challenges did Nathan face in becoming a successful actor? How were actors trained in the early theatre? What qualities and skills did they require?

(3) Why were Alleyn and Burbage so acclaimed?

(4) Why did the Puritans object to playhouses and plays?

(5) Why were actors regarded as vagabonds?

(6) Why were women not permitted to perform on the public stage?

(7) What was the place of the theatre in Jacobean London?

(8) What were the most popular themes of Jacobean plays?

(9) Why did Jacobean playwrights write satirical comedies?

(10) How did Jacobean playwrights try to evade censorship?

(11) Why did monarchs patronise companies of players?

(12) Why did the Jacobean court stage such extravagant masques?

(13) What caused the downfall of Nathan Field? Did he deserve it?

(14) What feelings did this book evoke for you?

(15) What aspects of Nathan's story could you most relate to?

(16) Which other character would have made an interesting protagonist?

(17) What other books by this author have you read? How did they compare to this book

SELECT BIBLIOGRAPHY

Primary Sources

John Aubrey, *Brief Lives* (The Boydell Press, 1993).

John Bulwer, *Chirologia or the natural language of the hand* (1644).

Samuel Daniel, *The vision of the twelve goddesses: a royal masque. Presented upon Sunday night, being the eight of January, 1604, in the greate hall at Hampton Court, and personated by the Queen's Most Excellent Majestie, attended by eleven ladies of honour* (1604) (ed Ernest Law, 1880).

Nathan Field, *The Plays of Nathan Field: Edited from the Original Quartos with Introductions and Notes* (Classic Reprint, 2019).

Richard Flecknoe, *Short Discourse of the English Stage* (Early English Books, 1604).

Thomas Fuller, *The History of the Worthies of England* (Nuttall and Hodgson, 1662).

Philip Henslowe, *The Diary of Philip Henslowe and The Life of Edward Alleyn*, Vol I (Elibron Classics, 1583).

Nicholas Rowe, *Some Account of the Life of Mr. William Shakespeare* (1709).

Sir Anthony Weldon, *The Court and Character of King James I,* (1650).

Secondary Sources

Julie Ackroyd, *Child Actors on the London Stage, Circa 1600: Their Education, Recruitment and Theatrical Success* (Sussex Academic Press, 2017).

David Bradley, *From Text to Performance in the Elizabethan Theatre: Preparing the Play for the Stage* (CUP, 1992).

Roberta Brinkley, *Nathan Field: The Actor-Playwright* (The Shoe String Press, 1993).

Judith Cook, *Roaring Boys: Shakespeare's Rat Pack* (Sutton Publishing, 2006).

Richard Dutton, "The Revels Office and the Boy Companies, 1600-1613: New Perspectives" (English Literary Renaissance, Vol. 32, No. 2, Studies in Drama and Culture (SPRING 2002), pp. 324-351).

G. Blakemore Evans, *Elizabethan-Jacobean Drama: The Theatre in its Time* (A&C Black, 1990).

Joy Leslie Gibson, *Squeaking Cleopatras: The Elizabethan Boy Player* (Sutton Publishing Limited, 2000).

Bernard Grebanier, *Then Came Each Actor* (David McKay Company, 1975).

Sarah Gristwood, *Arbella: England's Lost Queen* (Bantam Books, 2004).

Katherine Hudson, *Story of the Elizabethan Boy Actors* (OUP, 1971).

W. David Kay, *Ben Jonson: A Literary Life* (The Odyssey Press, 2017).

Edel Lamb, *Performing Childhood in the Early Modern Theatre: The Children's Playing Companies (1599-1613)* (Palgrave MacMillian, 2005).

Leanda de Lisle, After *Elizabeth: The Death of Elizabeth and the coming of King James* (Harper Perennial, 2006).

Clare McManus, *Women on the Renaissance Stage: Anne of Denmark and female masquing in the Stuart court 1590-1619* (Manchester University Press, 2002).

Lucy Munro, *Children of the Queen's Revels: A Jacobean Theatre Repertory* (CUP, 2011).

Lucy Munro, *Shakespeare in the Theatre: The King's Men* (Bloomsbury, 2021).

J.E. Neale, *Queen Elizabeth I* (Pimlico, 1998).

R.E. Pritchard ed, *Shakespeare's England: Life in Elizabethan and Jacobean Times* (The History Press, 2010).

James Shapiro, *1599: A Year in the Life of William Shakespeare* (Faber and Faber, 2005).

Michael Shapiro, *Children of the Revels: The Boy Companies of Shakespeare's Time and their Plays* (Columbia University Press, 1977).

Antonia Southern, *Player, Playwright, Preacher's Kid: The Story of Nathan Field, 1587 – 1620* (Athena Press, 2009).

Simon Thurley, *The Royal Palaces of Tudor England* (Yale University Press, 1993).

Steven Veerapen, *The Wisest Fool: The Lavish Life of James VI and I* (Birlinn Limited, 2023).

Eliane Verhasselt, "*A Biography of Nathan Field, Dramatist and Actor*" (Revue Belge de Philologie et d'Histoire, Année 1946 25-3-4 pp. 485-508).

Charles William Wallace, *The Children of the Chapel at Blackfriars, 1597-1603. Introductory to the children of the Revels, their origin, course and influences* (Leopold Classic Library, 2015).

Stanley Wells, *Shakespeare and Co* (Penguin, 2007).

Ethel Williams, *Anne of Denmark* (Longman, 1970).

Printed in Great Britain
by Amazon